Tales for Well-Dressed Cynics
and Optimistic Ragamuffins

Cathleen Davies

4 Horsemen
Publications, Inc.

Fluid
Copyright © 2023 Cathleen Davies. All rights reserved.

4 Horsemen Publications, Inc.
1497 Main St. Suite 169
Dunedin, FL 34698
4horsemenpublications.com
info@4horsemenpublications.com

Cover and Typesetting by Autumn Skye
Edited by Jen Paquette

All rights to the work within are reserved to the author and publisher. No part of this publication may be reproduced, stored in a retrieval system, or transmitted in any form or by any means, electronic, mechanical, photocopying, recording, scanning, or otherwise, except as permitted under Section 107 or 108 of the 1976 International Copyright Act, without prior written permission except in brief quotations embodied in critical articles and reviews. Please contact either the Publisher or Author to gain permission.

All characters, organizations, and events portrayed in this novel are either products of the author's imagination or are used fictitiously. All brands, quotes, and cited work respectfully belong to the original rights holders and bear no affiliation to the authors or publisher.

Library of Congress Control Number: 2023938102

Paperback ISBN-13: 979-8-8232-0203-9
Audiobook ISBN-13: 979-8-8232-0202-2
Ebook ISBN-13: 979-8-8232-0204-6

Dedication

To Frances and Josephine and Julie and all the formidable women who are mothers to formidable women.

Acknowledgements

I want to thank the University of Birmingham, and my supervisor C D Rose in particular, who helped me turn this vague idea into a passable MA thesis. Throwing myself into this project reminded me of all the things I love (music, art, bodies, community, filth, sex, poetry etc.), and that has kept me writing for far longer than I perhaps have any right to.

Many of these stories have already been published in various magazines and anthologies. I'd like to thank: *Storgy Magazine*, *Mercurius*, *The Bookends Review*, *The Fictional Cafe*, *Literally Stories*, and *Weasel Press*. Thank you for seeing the potential in my work during the baby stages and for helping each story find an independent home.

I feel it's important to show gratitude to all the artists and activists who fought to make my strange, queer life as exciting and free as it is now. Thank you to all the LGBTQIA+ people who had the gall to live their lives as fully and authentically as possible when the world was so relentlessly hostile towards them. Thank you to all the people who still do. Special thanks to Cosey Fanni Tutti who replied to my gushing email with helpful suggestions and unbelievable warmth during the writing process.

While certain characters have been inspired by real-life artists, they are definitely not those people and shouldn't be regarded as such. This work should be treated as what it is: a work of fiction.

Contents

Truism #1: Alienation produces
    eccentrics or revolutionaries 1
Cowboy T-Shirt Design 5
Truism #2: Children are the
    hope of the future 14
Post-Partum Document 17
Truism #3: Raise boys and
    girls the same way. 27
Rhythm 0 29
Truism #4: Often you should act
    like you are sexless 36
Menstruation Bathroom. 38
Truism #5: Decency is a relative thing 44
Prostitution 47
Truism #6: Labour is a
    Life-destroying Activity. 58
Mann & Frau & Animal 59
Truism #7: Anger or hate can
    be a useful motivating force 67
Through the Night Softly. 70

Truism #8: Romantic love was
 invented to manipulate women 77
Reading Position for Second-Degree Burn ... 79
Truism #9: Random mating is
 good for debunking sex myths 87
Oxidation Painting 89
Truism #10: Crimes against property
 are relatively unimportant. 97
Arthur Rimbaud in New York 101
Truism #11: You can't expect people
 to be something they're not 109
Untitled (Self Portrait with Blood) 113
Truism #12: Abuse of Power
 Comes as No Surprise 126
I'm too sad to tell you. 128
Truism #13: Turn soft and lovely
 anytime you have a chance 131
Blood Work Diary 135
Truism #14: The only way to be
 pure is to stay by yourself 146
Sang/ Lait Chaud. 150
Truism #15: The most profound
 things are inexpressible 161
Red Flag 163
Truism #16: All things are
 delicately interconnected 176
Frankie's Teardrop (A Review). 179

Works Cited 181
Book Club Questions 185
Author Bio 187

Truism #1:

Alienation produces eccentrics or revolutionaries

Judith heard the raucous laughter and the scrambling of keys which meant her daughter was finally home. She *had* been enjoying her book. The door opened and slammed shut. Dual footsteps thumped upstairs while meaningless chatter fell from Tracy's mouth like dribbled vomit,

"God, I'm *soaking* wet. Can you believe they had pistols?"

The mystery boy laughed along with her. Judith didn't recognise his voice.

"Um, Tracy!" she shouted.

"What?" Tracy yelled back from the top of the stairs.

"Don't speak to me through the wall, please. Come here."

"God's sake…"

Her daughter thumped back down the stairs and Judith couldn't help but be impressed by the fantastic amount of noise she could make on carpet. A painted head peeked round the living room door. Lipstick was smeared in stripes across her cheeks. Her hair was tied in scruffy plaits, a pigeon feather poking out from the twisted bobble. Judith cringed. *God, think of the germs.*

"Christ, what's on your face?" she asked.

"We're playing Cowboys and Indians," Tracy replied.

"And whose lipstick is that?"

Tracy thought it wise to stay quiet.

"Who's your friend?"

Another face peeked round the door. He was at least three years older than Tracy, all acne and red cheeks (which may have been embarrassment but might as easily have been smudged lipstick—who could tell?) Someone, presumably Tracy, had attempted to pull his hair into plaits too, but they barely reached his shoulder and looked ridiculous. Judith loved her daughter, but she didn't understand why she needed to befriend every oddball who stumbled across her path. She was pretty in a rough and tumble kind of way. She might have been popular if she tried.

"Hello, Mrs. Lamb," the youth said.

"Hello, love. And who are you?"

"It's *Nick*, Mum," Tracy said, as though that were obvious. Naturally, this was the first time Judith had ever heard of the boy.

"Right. And does your mother know you're here, Nick?"

Nick nodded, a tad too sheepishly. Clearly not then.

Acknowledgements

"And you're alright with that lipstick on, are you?" she asked him.

He shrugged. "It makes it more fun to pretend."

"Right. Well, it's been lovely meeting you, but it *is* a school night and our Tracy's already late back, which she knows isn't allowed. Besides, we'll be having our tea soon."

"Can't Nick stay for tea, Mum?"

"For God's sakes, Tracy. I've only two chops out."

"But Nick's mum never has anything in."

"Well, that sounds like Nick's mother's prerogative."

"Why are you always such a…?" Tracy stopped herself.

"Such a what, darling? You didn't finish there."

"Well, if Nick's not staying, I'm not either."

Tracy traipsed away dramatically (everything she did, she did dramatically), leading Nick away by the hand.

"You bloody well are not leaving, if you think you can just…" A door slammed. No laughter this time. Judith sat in a state of semi-amused shock. She would absolutely kill that girl when she got home. Honestly, she would. Still, she thought, resuming her book, she supposed it would be two lamb chops to herself tonight. That was a silver lining.

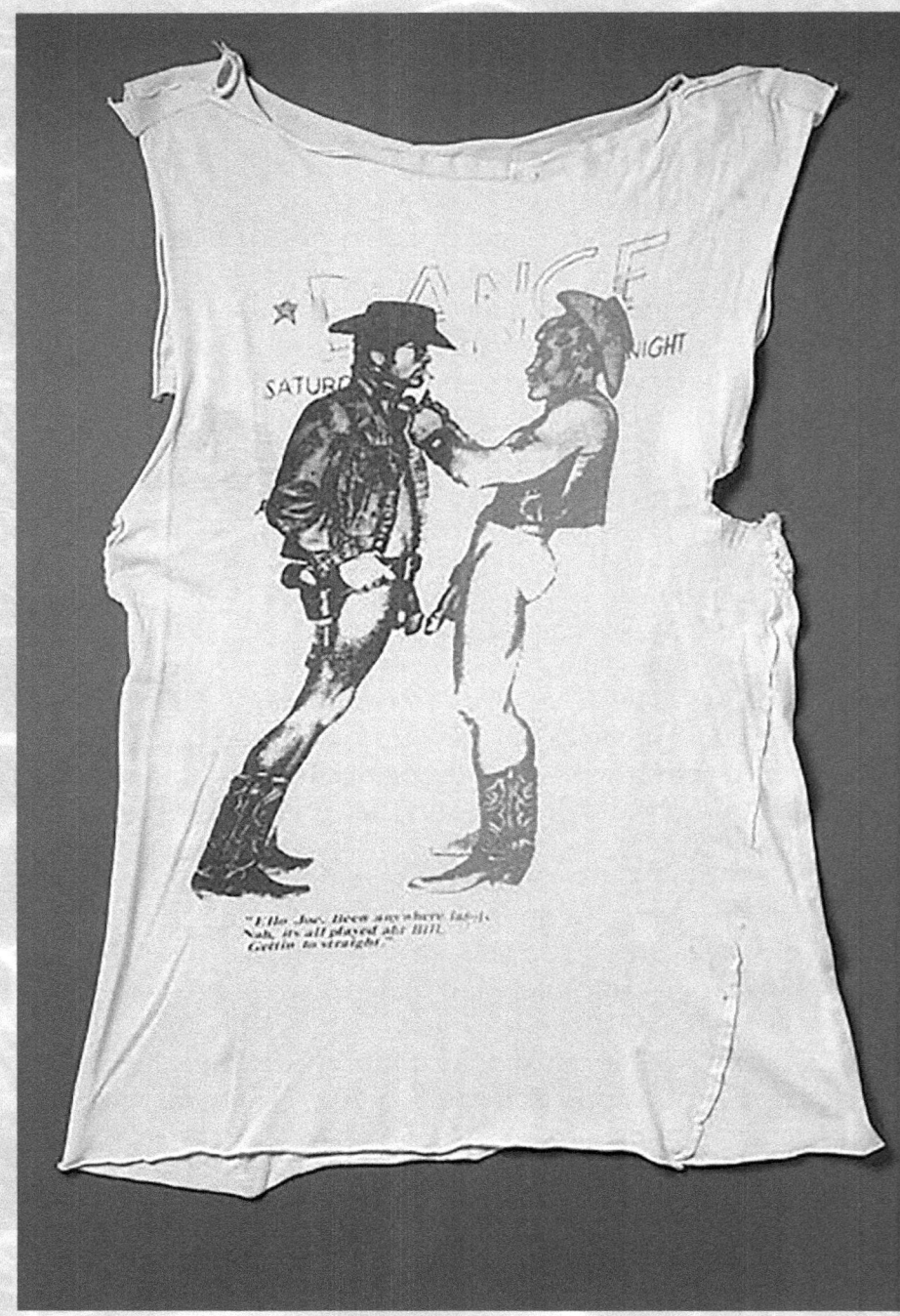

Nude Cowboy T-shirt by Malcolm McLaren and Vivienne Westwood for SEX" credit: Malcolm McLaren Estate.

Cowboy T-Shirt Design

There was blood in his underwear. Nick found it in the hotel bathroom, the floor mildly sprinkled with pubic hair, black mould lining the edge of the sink, but it was the blood that'd disgusted him the most. He could still taste the skin. It'd seemed so similar to old coins—a metallic, human flavour just like the blood now staining the whites of his pants—and Nick supposed that all these fluids probably tasted the same. A moment later, his vomit proved him wrong.

"You alright in there, cowboy?" Joe shouted through the bathroom door, and Nick knew he'd have that smirk on his face. That smirk was the closest Joe ever got to a smile, and Nick hated it even more than seeing him miserable.

He'd booked the room because he wanted to take it seriously. *Travelling with my son:* that's what he'd said in the lobby, his arm around Joe's shoulders, conscious of the perspiration clinging to his armpit. The room had two single beds and smelled like mothballs. The narrow hallways echoed with the sound of affairs.

The lobby didn't care what they were up to. Joe knew that. He'd seen enough people like him waiting around for lifts, smoking cigarettes. The illusion was all for Nick. Nick just *had* to take it all seriously.

In the back of his mind though, even Nick knew it was funny. Joe had stood there in his combat boots, the cowboy hat aslant, still in the leather vest that he refused to take off. It was the neckerchief that did it. The neckerchief really cemented the ridiculousness of their whole situation. Aside from the boots, they wore nothing on their bottom halves and whenever Nick got the chance, he caught a glimpse of Joe's flaccid cock.

"I guess it's not homo if you've got half your gear on." Joe had been smirking then too.

"Can you not?" Nick said.

"Not what?"

"Make jokes."

"Have you seen us?"

"I know, but still."

Nick didn't want to leave; he knew that. He wanted to be there, just like he'd wanted to be there all the other times, but he didn't want it to be happening to him. The costumes helped in that regard, but still, it wasn't perfect. Nick wished that he was trapped in a super-sensuous dream where he could feel everything that happened, see it all in crystal clarity, the crumple of the bedsheets in his fists, the leather rubbing on his back… then he'd wake up, shake his head at the strange dream, and mention it to no one. His wife would sleep on blissfully, not noticing a thing.

"Listen, cowboy, this was your idea."

Nick lit a cigarette although his throat was sore. Perhaps it was all the whisky he'd drunk, but he felt empty without a cigarette in his hands. He glanced up, noticed the ceiling was turning brown from tar and felt solely responsible.

"I know. I thought it would be cute. Sexy or something, I don't know. Maybe we should just get dressed," he said. Joe shrugged indifferently, and Nick wished that he'd at least pretend to care. "Help me with the neckerchief, though. I can't get it off. Never learned knots in the scouts, you know?"

"I didn't go to scouts," Joe said.

"They're American," Nick said, "like cowboys." He attempted a laugh which Joe didn't reciprocate. Instead, he moved to undo the knot.

And Nick caught his breath when Joe touched him. These small acts were always the most intimate of all. It wasn't the way he grabbed him or the tongue inside his mouth that caused the sharp intake of breath, the stomach flip. It was the way a hand would graze a knee and lips would brush past ears, the way they sometimes stood too close against a grimy bar pretending not to know each other, hairs standing on end. It was the way, just then, that Joe leant backwards with one eye closed as he untied the neckerchief, knuckles grating against stubble before catching his eye.

"It's undone."

That was when they'd started. Nick liked to think that Joe wanted this. That wasn't really the case, of course, but it would be the memory he'd force of it anyway. It's what he'd try to recollect.

It wasn't the first time someone had made him bleed. Nick got in a fair few scraps as a kid. His mum always told him he wouldn't get in trouble with her for fighting. *Someone makes you bleed, you make them bleed right back. That's how men should be.*

He'd tried to erase the slurred voice from his memories. Nick wasn't delusional. He just liked to soften the edges. The truth was arriving home from school had always smelt like whisky.

Joe understood this kind of love. Nick remembered how they'd met, Joe crying and bleeding on the pavement, no home to go back to, no mother to protect him. Nick couldn't go home either. He hated the way his wife looked so tired and miserable. He couldn't bear the thought of returning to her lying bloated on the sofa, desperate for affection. Instead, he drove around. He told Iris he had to work late, but he knew the places he could go if he wanted fun, knew enough people, though never by name. He never told anyone his name either; that was all part of it. There was theatre in the degeneracy. Iris didn't pay attention

Cowboy T-Shirt Design

to anything Nick did. She spent her time at book clubs reading up on women's lib, discovering the power of her own (wasted) female sexuality. Nick wasn't even sure the baby was his, but he liked his wife for two reasons: she didn't ask questions, and she didn't drink. She liked book clubs and expensive clothes, and with that, she was content. She'd never be happy. He heard her sobbing at night, clutching her swollen stomach. Nick reminded her often that many people had to make do with contentment.

Nick had met Joe when he was crying, face hidden beneath his greying t-shirt. In his attempt to wipe his tears, he'd stained the rim with blood. Nick crept along the curb, calling to him through wound-down window:

"Oi. Do you need to go to hospital?"

"No," Joe said, though it was obvious he did.

"Well do you need a lift home then? Your mother must be worried."

"Not got one."

"Which: a home or a mother?" Nick had intended it to be funny, but Joe's eyes filled more rapidly with tears. He buried his face in his quickly soaking t-shirt, exposing the skin of his lanky stomach to the cold. His dirty boots gave it away and the awkward, lumpy rucksack that was far too big to carry around casually. "Listen, hey, don't do that," Nick attempted. "Come on. Let me get you a pint at least."

Joe looked at him properly then, sizing him up. Eventually, he nodded. He really was angelic, tall and wide-eyed with a lanky frame and dimpled cheeks. It was a shame. In his scene, he'd be better off with pimples and rotting teeth.

"You look like you've been glassed," Nick said when Joe slammed the car door behind him. "That happened to me once too."

"You can do what you want, but you don't have to talk to me," Joe replied.

So it began.

Nick still felt unable to flush the vomit away, but he knew at some point he was going to have to leave. He'd leave Joe in the warm bed he'd rented for him, get back in his car, and drive home. He'd take off his suit for the second time that night and crawl into bed next to his oblivious wife. She would murmur something about it seeming late, and he'd moan about the factory and having to sort out some mess. Hopefully, she'd do the laundry and think nothing of the blood stain.

For some reason though, Nick couldn't stand up. There was a banging sickness in his head which felt similar to being glassed, and he knew what that felt like because the night his own mother threw a glass at him, he'd not managed to move in time.

Cowboy T-Shirt Design

Nick knew he was bleeding, but he didn't want to wipe it away. He was sixteen and dizzy and scared. He looked up at his mother, hoping that she'd see the blood, see his shocked expression and feel guilt, but she leant against the kitchen door frame smirking.

"I had to pay the bills," he said.

"Pathetic," she slurred at him, swaying ever so slightly. "Call yourself a man. Can't look after your own mum."

The blood dripped in his eye then. He was forced to wipe it away, felt astounded by the quantity of red seeping into the cracks on his fingers creating squiggled roads.

"I get paid at the beginning of the month," he said. "Until then, we have to make do."

His mother started nodding as though she were trying to understand, but her face was still twisted, cruel. He hated it when she was like this. She knew, he thought. She knew he'd hidden some money away for more shopping when they'd inevitably need it. He grabbed the dustpan and brush from the corner, kneeling down to start dealing with the shards.

"You don't think I know, but I do," she sneered.

And while Nick was brushing up the glass, he noticed his blood dripping on the floor and the way that brushing over it left bristly smears on the pale green tiles.

"I hear what they say about you. You can't hide anything from me."

Nick tried to pretend that she wasn't speaking, blocked it out as though it were a memory. He'd always been talented at twisting reality.

"Why've you never brought a lass home, ey?" she asked.

And perhaps it was because of all this twisting that Nick responded how he did. He knew for certain that he didn't plan what he was going to do. Somehow, the words of his mother came through, not redecorated or tidied-up, but in the exact way she'd spoken and intended them. *If someone makes you bleed, you make them bleed right back. That's how men should be.* And that night Nick followed his mother's instructions, then he left home and didn't come back.

Kneeling on the hotel floor, Nick wondered where she was now. With his head against the porcelain seat, he felt the tears slide down his face before he registered the sadness. He'd heard that she was sleeping rough these days. He hoped it wasn't true.

In the bedroom, Joe drank from the bottle, his eye on the bathroom door. Nick didn't like how Joe refused to use tumblers, and Joe didn't like Nick in general. He felt better now though, knowing that the worst was over, and Nick would soon head back to his wife (poor cow). After all the time he'd spent with Nick, Joe now felt cocky enough to smirk when he finally emerged from the bathroom, face looking like a come-down.

"What? Too painful to take a shit?" he said, and when Nick punched him in the cheek, he stumbled backwards only out of shock. "What the fuck?" he attempted before a whisky glass connected with his head. Joe fumbled around for a place to sit. He didn't fight back. Instead, he stared at Nick, scared, but mostly just confused. "Is this because of the tumblers?" he asked.

Nick started sobbing then. He fell to his knees, gripping the front of Joe's shirt. Joe ignored this, only touching his forehead to see if there was blood.

"I don't need you," Nick sobbed. "I'm a man."

"Okay."

"Don't leave me."

"Okay," Joe said. "Alright."

Nick swaddled himself inside Joe's t-shirt, feeling the thin body inside it stiffen and he wanted to apologise and say that he loved him, tell him that he didn't really want to make him bleed. He couldn't say that though. He wanted to, but he couldn't. It just sounded too much like his mother.

Truism #2:
Children are the hope of the future

Judith needed stitches. She'd been torn apart. The agony couldn't be put into words as much as people had tried with their analogies about watermelons and keyholes: the squeezing, pulsing, tearing, bleeding, shitting mess that was the miracle of life. Judith was on her own when she went into labour. No drugs for her, thank you very much. The pain was so intense she would have opted out if it were possible, but when she held the baby in her arms, Judith knew she'd never have to go through anything alone again.

Years of failed relationships had taught her that there was love in sweat and tears and blood, always an element of yourself left behind in the process of lovemaking. *A little death,* they called it. She looked at her baby's crinkled, scrunched-up eyes, her pink face, wrinkled little fingers. Skin on skin, Judith held her baby close to her, the baby coated in her own insides, being from her own insides, and she kissed the top of the fluid-coated head and knew that love came from blood and sweat and tears, but now it was real. This, for the first time, was unconditional.

"Hello, little one," Judith whispered. "Hello, Tracy."

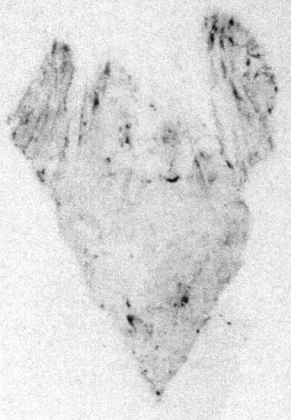

Mary Kelly
Post-Partum Document: Documentation I,
Analysed Faecal Stains and Feeding Charts, 1974
Perspex unit, white card, diaper linings,
plastic, sheeting, paper, ink
Detail, 1 of 31 units, 28 x 35.5 cm
Art Gallery of Ontario

Post-Partum Document

Susie Jones was pregnant. She was twenty-three, and it was her first. She'd broken the news to her husband while he was listening to the football game, and for some reason, she thought that was hilarious.

"How daft am I? Interrupting our Dave in the middle of footy. Can you imagine?" Susie told this story when she was seven months gone, slumped on Iris's sofa. Iris hadn't invited Susie Jones over. Iris hadn't seen anyone in months, but of course this get-together was all Karen Oaks's doing.

"She'd love to hear from you," Karen had said over the phone. "No one else has any babies. Don't get me wrong, we've all *had* babies, but it's not the same when they're grown, is it?"

"I suppose not."

"And how old is yours now, four months?"

"Five months," Iris said.

Fluid

"Ooh heck, dunnit just fly by?" And Iris hadn't responded because she didn't have anything to say.

Her little blue-eyed boy. That's what they called him, and Iris decided she'd best adopt that nickname too because she hadn't thought of one herself yet. She just called her baby "Nick." She didn't think that he looked like a Nicholas, although he did look remarkably like his father, and as his father was also called Nicholas, she supposed that, actually, he must. Remarkable really was the word for it. They had the same square jaw, the same beady eyes, the same screwed-up mouth, always so small unless he was bawling, which set her teeth on edge.

Iris didn't know how to stop him crying. She'd just never learned. She cuddled and kissed, spoke in a sing-song voice, rocked him gently, but it never worked. It was like he hated her, but then he needed her so desperately that she couldn't possibly leave. Who would love her then? The mother who left her own child? No, Nick was too intelligent for that. He knew as soon as he was born she'd have no choice but to accept his love and his alone. Eventually, when the cuddles and kisses proved entirely ineffectual, she would be forced to do it. She'd pull down her bra and allow him to grip onto her with his teething, gaping mouth, making her squirm as the liquid drained from her, experiencing that same nausea that she felt when doctors took her blood. It was worth all the pain and the heavy breasts just to avoid that feeling of being sucked at for a few more moments.

Now Susie Jones sat on her dirty fabric sofa next to Karen Oaks, and Iris wanted to cry, but she wasn't sure why, so she didn't. The three of them smoked their cigarettes and cooed over Nick squirming on Iris's lap. Soon, his face changed. In came the screwed-up expression which meant he wanted to cry soon too, and Iris didn't know why he wanted to do that either.

"Oh, I think someone's hungry," Karen Oaks said the second he started fussing, and soon his mouth was wide-open, wet and threatening.

"Aw, can I watch? It's so beautiful, that bond, you know?" Susie interjected.

"No," Iris said quickly. "I don't think so."

"G'on, it's only us girls. I used to whap 'em out all over the shop when our Ian was a bairn. It was the only way I could ever stop him scriking. Course, he'd start pulling 'em out *for* me if I didn't get there fast enough," Karen said, and the two women laughed together while Iris sat there, self-pityingly, alone. She recognised the sinking sensation in her stomach which signalled that soon she would have to do something she didn't want to do, but which was required to maintain her illusion of normality.

"I just don't think he's hungry," she attempted. "I fed him before you came."

"We've been here ages."

"Well, he ate a lot."

Fluid

The cries were getting more insistent, and Iris knew what she looked like. She could tell by the doubtful expressions on their faces. They would speak about her afterward. *Bad mother*, they would say, *didn't even seem to care that he was crying, left him starving hungry, poor thing.* Iris would never be able to defend herself because the way she felt was undefendable.

"He does seem upset," Susie Jones attempted cautiously.

"Well, you know bairns. Suppose sometimes they cry for no reason..."

"I'll feed him," Iris said, too quickly, to the point that they would know she was annoyed, and she tried to recover with a warm smile, but she just looked mad with her sudden teeth-baring expression. Iris imagined herself as an animal. A pig, perhaps, or a dog laid on its side passively while its young audibly nibbled on sagging, brown nipples. Iris cautiously withdrew her breast, tried to keep the nipple hidden but failed, as she knew she would. She smiled awkwardly, hoping that they wouldn't notice her embarrassment, but Karen Oaks and pregnant Susie Jones still had their eyes fixed on her bawling son.

He clenched on quickly and began sucking, and Iris felt her anger grow with each insistent slurp. *You bastard*, she thought. *Could you not have pretended for at least a second?*

"My goodness," Susie said, "isn't it beautiful?"

Post-Partum Document

"You do miss it in a strange way," Karen Oaks added. "I definitely miss the bond I had with mine."

"Does it really go away?" Susie asked.

"No, of course not, but it's not the same, is it? When they're in their teens and only bothered about Top of the bloody Pops. You miss them even though they're still technically there."

"Oh, everyone says that though, don't they? Grow up so fast."

Iris felt her eyes prick with tears. This was expected. She'd been like an overhanging, grey cloud waiting to burst the entire time these women had been here, watching her and her son, waiting for her to slip up. She wondered how she could feel so guilty and angry all at the same time, and over such a tiny, little child. The anger made her think she was a terrible person, built up the guilt she knew she was supposed to feel. In turn, that guilt made her anger more apparent, because why should she feel guilty? She'd never agreed to any of this. She'd never had a say in marriage and children. How could she possibly be expected to cope? This anger grew into guilt at being angry into anger at being guilty into an exhausting, overwhelming sensation that left her numb, blank, responding only when she had to so she wouldn't feel too much.

Iris had never been fond of children. Her parents were. They'd wanted four or five but only managed one in fifty years of marriage. They called Iris their "little miracle." Whenever they saw a baby, they would speak in an absurd language, goo-gaaing and gaa-gooing nonsense at an indifferent and confused face. They made bizarrely specific comments to strangers about the beauty of their children, always insisted on getting maddeningly involved in school events. Iris had found it humiliating to see them waving at every sports day, shouting out her name from the crowd. Even as an adult, she found the whole thing embarrassing. All that sick and piss and shit, the screaming, the total disregard for etiquette. Familial love evaded her.

They said it would be different when she had her own, and it had been, in a way. There was so much love there when she saw that big, square face of his. Sometimes she watched Nick while he slept, and it was painful, physically painful, to feel how much she loved him. It overwhelmed her so much she would stand over his crib and sob, silent tears falling in drops off the bottom of her chin. She'd think about how it was so strange that their faces scrunched up in the same way, and that very thought would make her hands clasp tighter on the pillow while he looked so sweet and peaceful, imagining a life where he'd never have to feel the way she felt right now. Of course, she'd never do it. But then, she couldn't ever be too sure. Both the Nicks would sleep through this. No one ever woke when Iris cried.

"Oh love," Karen said, "don't get upset."

"You'll still have him forever," Susie said. "But bless her, in't she sweet?"

"Yes, it's hard to think of them ageing." Those words were wrong, and Iris knew it. These women would know that "ageing" was not why she was crying.

"Don't be sorry, love. It's emotional, especially when they still breast-feed."

At this point, Iris had stopped feeding him. She handed him back to Karen Oaks, feeling sickened as she tucked herself away. The pain in her breast had subsided, but she knew it would come back soon. She asked them to watch him while she put on the kettle.

"Tea, was it? Or Coffee?" She made a joke about being too tired to remember anything these days and her friends laughed, more sympathetic now that they'd seen her being milked.

"Oh, I guess I have that to look forward to," Susie said, "that and the sleepless nights, oh and the night feedings, and our Dave's no use, don't know how to change a bloody nappy, and thanks, by the way, Karen, for the clothes. In't that sweet, Iris? Karen gave me so many things she doesn't need. Shoes, bottles, clothes, the lot."

"Well, as mums, you quickly learn how to share."

"No space for it in the house, I suppose. Still, it's impossible to shop with Dave's limp."

And as they talked, Iris vaguely noticed herself disassociating, felt her mind leave her body while these women joked about the cuteness of small shoes and the sweetness of soft blankets with faded, yellow ducks, and dilation, and stitches, and all those screams of agony, and the exhaustion of it all, and how it was so sweetly cute, so cutely sweet, just so god-damned adorable, even down to the shit-stained clothes and dirty nappies.

"Speaking of which," Karen called through to the kitchen, "it might be time for someone to be changed."

Iris normally changed him on the living room floor, and she would've done it there and then, but somehow she felt ashamed to let them see it, smell it, didn't want them to think any less of him. Nick's shit was tough to clean. It stained his baby-grows a filthy yellow round the legs. Her house always smelled like shit now. It was one of the first things Karen said when she'd walked in, "I remember that new-baby smell," while Susie wrinkled up her nose.

Iris laid him on the kitchen table, the only surface free of dirty plates. The sink was piling up now too. Iris looked at all the grime, wishing emptily that it would go away. She hardly ever remembered eating, let alone cooking, so she wondered how it always got so filthy. She unbuttoned his baby-grow at the crotch and pulled it over his head. He whimpered while he was undressed. She figured it was the hardness on his back, perhaps the cold, but even then she couldn't help but feel irritated, then horrendously ashamed of her own irritation. Over his whimpers and cries, Iris continued to hear the all-knowing voice of Karen Oaks.

Post-Partum Document

"You know when mine was this age…"

Iris looked at the yellow sludge in his nappy. It had been flattened by his bum-cheeks into a butterfly with round, flat wings, and Iris, for a second, thought she might just love it. She imagined this might be symbolic, this butterfly. This shit-stain indicated a fresh beginning. He would have a clean nappy on soon, and the kitchen would be clean again in time. She would bake her husband cakes, and he wouldn't feel the need to work so late to avoid her, driving around town doing God knows what. Iris wouldn't let herself think about these things. She wouldn't worry. She would be a good mother, and she'd learn to embrace the sucking on her breasts, and all the talk of blankets and tiny shoes, and baby Nick would hardly ever cry because he'd know his mother loved him very much.

"How you getting on in there, love?" Karen Oaks had asked, and Iris replied:

"Beautifully," as she spread out the used nappy and decided that pregnant Susie Jones deserved to see the truth, the real art behind this whole thing, motherhood.

"Look," she said to both of them, walking back through to the living room. "Isn't this so special?" and she laughed slightly as she spoke, her eyes still wet with tears as she held the nappy out to them. But Susie Jones and Karen Oaks just stared at her. At first, their eyebrows raised, looking appalled, before they turned away. Iris felt her confidence waver. She wanted to explain her thoughts so that they'd understand that this did matter, that this was a breakthrough, and things would be good now.

"Look," Iris said, realising that she was nearly sobbing. "Look, you're not looking properly."

In the next room, baby Nick kept crying spread out on the kitchen table.

Truism #3:
Raise boys and girls the same way

Judith wasn't going to buy her one of those *dolls*. No chance. If she tried to pick a *Barbie*, Judith wasn't holding back. She'd tell her that the waist was unrealistically thin, the breasts unnaturally large, and the disproportionate nature of her figure would likely snap a real woman's spine. Judith let her Trace know exactly how much women were worth beyond the limits of unrealistic beauty standards. She'd talk about all those women who'd fought for her right to be something more than a silly, plastic wife who only aims to look pretty and act amenable and…

"Mum, can I have this?"

Tracy was, in fact, already bouncing on the space hopper. She had pulled up her skirt so that her knickers were on full display as she hopped right down the middle of the aisle.

"Why do you want that?" Judith asked.

Tracy shrugged. "It's fun." She spun around and turned the corner.

"Tracy, come back here, please…" Judith managed to say, a millisecond before she heard her knock over a full display of greetings cards. Her daughter's clumsiness beggared belief.

"Whoops," Tracy managed half-heartedly.

"Jesus Christ," Judith sighed to herself. "Why can't you just get a fucking doll?"

Rhythm 0

Joe doesn't know him, and that doesn't matter. He hopes it won't hurt, but it probably will. How long has this been going on for now? Six months? Seven? Joe knows that the weather was warm when he started, and now it's much colder. He's more willing to get into people's cars when it's cold. Perhaps that's a good thing.

It was easier in the beginning when he was begrudgingly accepting persistent offers, eventually giving in and taking as much money as he could get. He managed to hold onto a sense of self-respect then. Now, he had to solicit. He found people who looked like they might want it, cautiously sidled up to them, and hoped they wouldn't punch him in the face. At first, he believed the humiliation of their rejections would never leave him, but it did. Eventually, it all left him.

Tonight, it isn't a hotel, which is a shame because hotels are at least comfortable. It isn't the back of a car or a filthy toilet stall either, both of which are uncomfortable, but at least then Joe knows there's a time limit. Joe always takes half the money up front, so he doesn't care if they're caught in the act and have to scarper. It's safer. Safer, but uglier too. Tonight it's a house, and that scares him. Being in a house means this person doesn't have anything to hide. The John's good-looking. Good-looking people don't really have to pay unless they want to keep something discreet, which usually means something gross or painful. Joe is tired. He struggles to keep his eyes open.

"Can I request a rundown of your services?" the punter asks, inspecting his fingernails theatrically. Joe shrugs.

"You can do what you want to me."

"*To* you. I assumed it would be me getting something *from* you seeing as I'm the one paying." His chest hair pokes out from the unbuttoned collar, thick and wiry, different from his moustache. Joe shrugs again.

"Whatever."

"Anything I like, huh?"

Whenever Joe does this, he likes to put his mind elsewhere. "Anything."

If the John's hands are cold, Joe remembers school, and the way kids packed their snowballs hard into ice, and the teachers went mad if you even got *close* to one of their cars. He remembers lying with his brothers and sisters in bed and the way the little ones used to warm up their freezing feet on his legs, and he pretended that he hated it but didn't really mind because he already had *his* feet on his big sister behind him. He thinks about the whisky he poured down his throat on bonfire night where he and his friends were all huddled up on the climbing frame at the kiddies' playpark, cheering whenever they saw a flash of pink or green (ooooooh, ahhhhh…).

But Joe doesn't like to think about whisky anymore.

When they force him to his knees, he thinks about skinned knees from playing bulldog in the playground. He's sure that all his friends at one point lived freely with pebbles embedded in their skin. He remembers warm water being poured over the cuts to clean them, and being told by teachers that he was very brave because he never cried. He thinks about the game they played with conkers, smashing them against each other, remembering the number of their victories *"Mine's a twelver," "Yeah? Well, mine's a sixty-niner."* Back then, his pockets were always full of circular necessities: conkers, marbles, one-penny sweets… Joe used to bite gobstoppers in half as a party trick. Everyone else would still be sucking them, saliva gathering in their mouths and dribbling over their fingers as they continuously plucked them out to show everyone the changing colours, but Joe just bit into them, and everyone would groan. He wishes he hadn't done that so much. A lot of his teeth are loose now, and that worries him.

When they hurt him, he thinks about his grandmother's heavy hand whenever he was caught stealing (which was often) and his old girlfriend and how she used to thump him on the leg if he didn't pay her enough attention. He thinks about lots of things that aren't related to what's happening, and for the moment, that makes it okay. But then it always seems to last a lot longer than he thinks he can stand, and there's no way to measure the time passing unless they're playing music. If they're at a club, he counts the songs and guesses how long he must have been going. When they aren't playing songs, he has to listen to the heavy breathing, and he thinks about how he used to run everywhere until his chest would hurt and he'd taste something like iron in the back of his throat. When you think about it, you realise you never see little kids just walking. They always have the energy to run everywhere, and Joe wants to grab them and say: "*Oi, idiot, what the fuck are you running for?*"

But he doesn't know. It's hard to tell. If you asked him if he wanted to go back and do everything differently, he probably still wouldn't. Joe doesn't like to think about where he's ended up. It depresses him to consider how wary he is, how uncertain about the future. And where's he going to end up next? Dying on the streets, a needle sticking out his eyeball? Is he going to get killed one day? (Usually, that only happens to the ones who look like girls, but Joe understands that Johns think they know what they want, then kill you when you give it to them). But if someone told him, "Go back in time. Apply yourself. Get a

Rhythm 0

job, wear a suit, meet a wife," would he take the opportunity? Joe doesn't think so. As much as his life is a pain most of the time, he has his friends. He has the taste of sour beer and all the speed he needs to keep him jumping up and down on nights in pent-up, sweaty crowds. Sometimes, more sparingly these days but it still happens, he gets these moments of pure ecstasy, the hours and hours of lying down that pass by just like seconds. He used to like fucking for pleasure, but he doesn't do much of that now.

The thing is, when they have to pay for it, even the softest of kisses feel like disgusting slops. Quick, breathless primality becomes repulsive, not sexy. The worst parts are when Joe feels the shiver down his back, the blood rushing down that lets him know that outside of his control, he's enjoying this (how the fuck could he be enjoying this?), and it only happens sometimes, but it happens.

Tonight, there's no risk of him enjoying it.

Joe doesn't know why they like hurting him. He doesn't want the tears to spring up in his eyes, but they do. He was right to worry. This prick in his stupid, silk shirt thinks he's from the 1800s, this sexy vampire, this irresistible demon, fucking whatever. He bites Joe's neck far too hard. Joe doesn't understand how anyone would enjoy this or why that bloke thinks he might too. He's standing behind Joe, unbuttoning his trousers. It's hard to do it one-handed, but when Joe tries to help him, he slaps his hand away. Meanwhile,

Fluid

he's scrambling on the desk for something. Joe doesn't know what he's looking for. He hopes it's a Johnny. No. The punter grabs this stupidly outdated letter opener, and he's holding it by Joe's neck, tracing it casually across his throat (a pathetic attempt to be sensual, maybe?) and all the time growling nonsense in his ear.

"If you don't want me to hurt you, you'd better do what I say." Joe doesn't want to indulge in this. It's pointless. He's already told him he'll do what he wants. He manages a nod. "Good."

Considering the big song and dance, the actual act doesn't last too long. The guy holds the letter opener the whole time which keeps Joe on edge. When it's over, Joe stumbles forward, grabbing his trousers.

"Oh, I didn't say we were done," the man says. He's panting still, smiling slightly.

Telling people they can do whatever they want to another human and no one's going to come by to stop them should lead to a billion different reactions. It doesn't though. More often than not, it leads to pain. People like inflicting pain. Or maybe it's just the people Joe meets. The man drags the blade across Joe's stomach, and it breaks the skin harshly. He licks it off, taking something from him that Joe never wanted to give (although he supposes he did promise him everything). He watches this stranger lapping him up and feels horrible. It happens a few more times. Practically, Joe doesn't know how he's going to keep the cuts clean. He barely manages to keep himself clean when he's in one piece. If they get infected, what's he going to do?

It's getting late now. Joe's stomach is stinging, and in a way, it feels cathartic because he can focus on that pain instead. The man holds his torso as they go again, and Joe thinks his palms are insanely sweaty until he realises that it's his blood that's making their connection feel so wet. Joe bites his lip. It'll be over soon, he hopes.

Truism #4:
Often you should act like you are sexless

"Tracy!"

"Mother!"

"Don't you *dare* be sarcastic. Now is not the time."

"Oh bloody hell, what did I do now? Did I breathe in an inflammatory tone? Stand too close to the wrong crowd for a microsecond?"

"You ought to start putting away your own laundry."

"Is that it? I'll do it next time. God…"

"Because I found this in your drawers. Care to explain?"

"Oh. Well, they're not drugs if that's what you think…"

"I know exactly what they are."

"Then you don't need me to explain then, do you?"

"Who is he?"

"Who's who?"

"Don't be snide with me, young lady. Whoever it is."

"No one! It's a precaution. All the girls are on it these days."

"Oh yes, because you've always been such a sensible and *precautious* young girl?"

"Ooft, good one."

"Neighbours talk, you know? If they knew you were this sort of girl…"

"As opposed to the type that gets pregnant out of wedlock?"

"…"

"…"

"…"

"Alright, I'm sorry."

"Get out."

"What?"

"Out."

"Are you serious?"

"Do I look like I'm joking?"

"Fuck's sake. You know what? Fine."

Menstruation Bathroom

Their school shirts had turned a funny colour again because a footy sock had got tangled up in the scruff pile that was their bedroom floor. Karen supposed that these things happened. She wasn't all that angry, but she'd pretend she was so that the boys believed they were running her ragged. Then if she got *really* angry, she could completely let go, and instead of them being surprised at the outburst they'd squirm guiltily, believing that it was the *last straw* that had broken her instead of her notoriously short temper. It'd worked as a parenting technique so far. Her lads were terrified of her: a sure sign of respect.

Karen hung the washing on the shower rail. Normally it would go in the courtyard but it'd been chucking down before, and despite an encouraging burst of sunlight, Karen didn't trust that it'd stay dry. She hung up the murky-green school shirts while shaking her head, muttering, *"Dear, oh dear, oh dear…"* hoping her offspring

Menstruation Bathroom

might overhear and feel guilty (Ha! Like that would ever happen). Tragically, a pair of her knickers had been caught in the staining, and while she had no problem with sending the lads off to school looking like mucky pups, she had a bit more dignity for herself, thank you. Into the rubbish they went.

As in the bathroom bin, she saw it. Clear as day.

Now, it couldn't be her own because Karen was a woman of class and dignity. She wrapped *hers* up nicely in tissue so that when she disposed of them no one would know. This one was left loose and unravelling, as long and imposing as a turd. Karen cast her mind back. Who'd been round recently? Could it be one of her lot? But no, she'd had a proper clean of the bathroom on the Sunday afternoon just before she went out to book club.

Ah. Book club. Every Sunday evening. She always made sure to tell her lads, "Now you mind you behave while I'm gone." When she came back, she'd find they hadn't moved and were still staring dead-eyed at the television as though time hadn't passed at all. It had been that way for *years*. Now they were bringing girls back, apparently. She'd wring their bloody necks.

"PAUL. IAN!" she shouted at the top of her lungs. No movement. Typical. A house the size of a shoebox, and they still pretended they were deaf to the bloody world. Karen stomped across the hallway and kicked open their bedroom door. They heard her then alright.

"Jesus," Ian said. They'd both been lying on their single, perpendicular beds, Ian on his stomach, Paul on his back. Ian was doing homework, or else he'd set himself up to look like he was doing homework. Paul was just lying there. For hours, he could lie down, not sleeping exactly, but not doing anything of worth either. Sometimes he threw a tennis ball, up and down, up and down, staring at the poster of George Best he'd blue-tacked to the ceiling. Karen often wondered what was going on in that empty head of his to allow for such a constant aura of calm.

"Who's had a girl over?" she began.

"What?"

"I don't want any arguing. I just want to know which one of you has had a girl over." They both looked at each other with their eyebrows raised. Either they were genuinely confused or else trying to send panicked messages to each other about how to handle the situation. Karen held back, knowing that silence was often more effective than screaming.

"What girl?" Paul ventured bravely.

"Don't you start that with me, young man. I know there was a girl here."

Quiet. There was confusion on both their faces, and Karen wondered if she might have been mistaken. Paul's eyes were vacant and befuddled, but that didn't necessarily represent any kind of innocence. It was just as likely he'd forgotten impregnating some trollop as that he hadn't done anything wrong. Still, he was of that age, and for

Menstruation Bathroom

reasons inexplicable to Karen, girls did tend to like him. All of her instincts were telling her that Paul was the culprit, and she glared at him unfalteringly until in her periphery she noticed something about Ian's eyes.

Ian. Just fourteen. Serious, quiet, shy. She hadn't expected him to be out on the pull for a while yet, but he was shifty, looking down, his pencil scribbling on the page, colouring in his margins when he usually liked to be so neat.

"Ian," she said, "look up now."

He did, his eyes practically welling up already, the big softy. Karen had him, and she knew it. She let the silence speak for itself.

"It was just to do homework! And we didn't do anything…"

"I bloody knew it!"

Soon the truth came out. Karen knew the lass. Charlotte Bulger. She would grow up to be pretty no doubt, but right now, she was a plain Jane with spots and thick milk-bottle glasses. Her hair always needed a brush. That's what Karen thought whenever she saw her. Still, she had good bones. You could go far with good bones.

If she thought about it for a minute or two, Karen was thrilled. She'd been worried about Ian. He was into all that girly music, those lads that wore make-up and catsuits. He hadn't seemed interested in courting, and Karen didn't want to think what *that* could mean. Charlotte was a nice girl, too. She did very well in school. Frankly, Ian could do a lot worse.

Fluid

Ultimately, this was incredible news. Course, she couldn't let him know that.

"Right. Grounded. Two weeks. No telly. And if I catch you with a girl here again, then that'll be the end of it. You'll be walloped out this house faster than you can say, 'I didn't do it.' Do you understand me?"

Ian nodded slowly, his eyes still on the book.

"I said, 'Do you understand me?'"

"Yes, Mum," he interrupted before she'd finished, irritation edging into his tone.

"Right then."

She looked over at Paul. He was smiling in a smug little way, enjoying not being the one in trouble for a change. That wouldn't do.

"And you!" She pointed at him.

"Me?"

"What did you do with your football socks?"

"My what?"

Karen threw her green-tinted pants at him. "What do you call this?"

"Urgh, Mum..." He groaned as though she'd thrown her own excrement.

"Right, you can do the laundry for a month if you're not going to make my job easy for me. You got that?"

"Aw, come on..."

Karen slammed the door. Her work was done. She smiled. It was sweet to know her boys were growing up, running off with girls, doing their own washing. It was nice too, to know that she was close enough to them to be able to talk about these things. Behind the door, she heard Ian's desperate whisper.

"How did she *know,* though?"

Ah, sweetheart, she thought, returning to empty the bathroom bin. *Call it women's intuition.*

Truism #5:
Decency is a relative thing

"Honestly, Karen, you should've seen her. She was so bloody pleased with herself."

"Well, I suppose she knew it would wind you up, love."

"And she was bright enough for school, you know!"

"Ay, she's not thick."

"And of course, she thinks it's all a 'performance,' and she's an 'artist.' I mean, please."

"Call it what you like. It's downright lechery."

"And I mean, I'm not being funny, Karen, but I went to university. I've read the books. Do you know how hard it were for me in them days? I had to *fight to* be taken seriously."

"Testament to yourself, love."

"And this is what she throws herself away on?"

"I'm glad I've got lads. Couldn't be doing with this nonsense."

"And God, if you could've seen her face…"

"Suppose she thinks she's clever."

Menstruation Bathroom

"She *thinks* she's being a *feminist*. She's more like a bloody prostitute."

PROSTITUTION Poster. Coum Transmissions. 1976.

Prostitution

It was the tail-end of summer, warm enough that the girls were comfortable bare-breasted, but chilly enough that their nipples stiffened to pink and brown points. Gypsy stood dancing, her arms held high above her, turning first her wrists and then the rest of her body, her head lolling to her porcelain chest. Tracy danced with her, following her movements with a hint of the sardonic. Creep was naked from the waist down, stroking himself casually, eyes rolled back, his imagination enchanting him more than the girls ever could.

Then there was Joe. He was still fully dressed and sitting silently, indifferent to these paganesque celebrations. There was no denying it at this point. Revelations had to find the boy a sense of purpose.

Rev sat sober on her throne of cushions, observing the artists mingling on the floor in front of her. Their turntable played the antagonising music they'd all either helped create or else wished they had. They looked so young and hopeful, swaying blissfully along to the sounds, humming under their breath to a tune that didn't quite exist yet. Rev loved them. They were her children, and this was their haven, but this new boy seemed confused at best and downright hostile at worst.

Rev didn't believe in age, but she imagined she must be nearing her fifties. She didn't believe in gender either which was made abundantly apparent by the way she dressed in skirts and lingerie despite her stocky, six-foot frame, the jawline she didn't attempt to blend away. She did, however, believe in power structures, and so she meticulously watched over her community in what they all assumed was a profoundly meditative state.

"What do you do?" Gypsy had asked Joe, melting her head down onto his lap dizzily when she had tired of dancing. Her eyes sparkled in a way that might have indicated eccentricity but was more realistically the influence of psychedelics.

"Nothing," he'd said.

"I don't mean as a job, numpty." She laughed. "Art, music, poetry…?" She reached up to trace her finger over his nose, brushing her knuckles gently against his cheek.

"I don't do anything." He scowled, almost flinching away, and Rev wondered why he didn't push her off if he was irritated. Joe seemed to have no boundaries with touch, which meant the artists adored him despite his less-than-sunny disposition and gathered around to paw at him like cats near a soft blanket. An angelic-looking teenager willing to be held and touched would always bode well for morale, and Rev initially found this justification enough for including him.

"You have to do something," Gypsy had persisted.

"I don't."

"What he *does* is look drop ... dead ... gorgeous." Tracy squatted down and crawled towards them from the other side of the circle. "And he lets us take pictures of him."

She leant over Gypsy to kiss Joe on the mouth. When she pulled away, his eyes were closed, the corners of his mouth turned up in such a way that, if Rev didn't know any better, could have been considered a smile. This informed Rev that Joe was probably in love with Tracy, and that they were almost definitely fucking. That might have been a cause for concern, but it wasn't; Rev had faith that Tracy could break hearts.

It did seem about the right time for Joe to fall in love. He pretended to be terrifying with all those spikes and safety pins, but Rev could see that he was a sensitive boy. Gypsy pretended not to notice the kiss, instead deciding to make waves in the air with her hand.

"He'll write for us," Rev intervened. "Some kids want to review our show but won't publish *my* interpretations. Joe has their sort of look. He can do it."

"What?" Joe looked as though he'd been insulted. "I can't write."
"Everyone writes. They demand it of children in school."
"I don't, though," Joe said, and Gypsy started stroking his knee while he pretended not to notice. "I can't spell."
"Good!" Rev insisted. "I've personally always found standardised British spelling to be restrictive."
This wasn't something Rev had always found, but she decided to pretend it was if it moved the situation along. The group would be performing soon, and any publicity was good publicity. Rev's own scripts were often treated with scorn, written off as self-indulgent and conceited (which they were, and she couldn't understand why this was so thoroughly disapproved of). When critics wrote about their group, Rev found they either lacked understanding, which bothered her, or expressed pure outrage, which delighted her but negatively impacted their funding. At any rate, the utilisation of forgotten, street children couldn't possibly hurt their already questionable reputation, and Rev saw no reason not to use Joe as a vessel. She'd heavily edit the review later, get across her own explanations while Joe's self-esteem grew from the feeling of inclusion and accomplishment. Before Joe could protest further, Tracy was kissing him again.
It wasn't surprising that Joe and Tracy were fucking because everyone was, often and loudly,

Prostitution

so much so that after a few weeks in the squat, Joe began to sleep better with the sounds of rhythmic thumping in the same way those in big cities grew accustomed to traffic noise. Rev was always happy to participate in such group activities. She slept with people in her office, which was really a bedroom, which was really an open art-space because she didn't like to give things labels. It was the smallest room in the squat, and the artists had helped to cover it in bunting and paint, cloth flowing from the ceiling so it looked like the inside of a circus tent. Their slogans were graffitied on the walls (an old habit from Rev's university days), and there was little room for much, excepting piles of clothes and trinkets the artists brought to Rev as gifts. It was rare she got through the day without Bridlington seashells, lost children's gloves, used tampons, snapped guitar strings, a medley of potential inspiration handed to her for the taking. Rev appreciated them as mothers appreciate hand-drawn portraits from their children. The bed didn't have a frame nor mattress and was instead an abundance of pillows and blankets, always stained and musty with the fragrances of sweat and scented candles. Throughout the squat, the distinct smell of sweat permeated, and this gave it its primality, reminding all the artists that they were still alive.

 Joe liked to sleep in Rev's bed sometimes. On his first night, he'd tried to sleep *with* her, put his hand on her thing (he wasn't sure if he should call it a cock, but it was definitely a thing) and started to lazily rub. He was exhausted, wasn't sure how many days he'd been awake, and looked forward to the sleep which would inevitably come quickly and hopefully soon. Rev lit a cigarette.

"Darling, I'm not sure you're really invested in this."

Had he been more awake, Joe would have raised his head.

"Why'd you bother inviting me then?"

"I didn't *invite* you. This place is here, and all are welcome to join it. I simply showed you the way inside."

Rev considered telling him that he could leave at any time but decided against it. It sounded far too cult-like, and besides, there was always the risk that he would actually leave before Creep had managed to take pictures of him. Rev had seen the welts on his buttocks, the scars on his stomach, the cigarette burns on his chest. With his injuries and arresting, blue eyes, Joe would undoubtedly take a good picture. Creep would adore the mixture of beauty and damage, the artistic juxtaposition this boy held.

She needn't have worried about Joe leaving. By the time Rev turned her head, wondering at the lack of response, Joe was already asleep with his hand still resting unthinkingly on her. He would stay in the commune, sulking and indifferent, for months.

Prostitution

The show went well, and Rev knew this because it was criticised tremendously.

Music played through overhead speakers during the proceedings. At first, it started as back-masked children's songs, the effect deliberately nauseating, and every voyeur's shoe-step echoing on the wooden floor effectively demonstrated their discomfort. People walked around the theatre as though they were being followed, occasionally stopping to let their invisible stalker overtake while conveniently at a display of homoerotic fabric weavings, bloodied tissues, or photographs of black and white execution victims. During the performance, when the audience was tentatively perched on their seats, Kum By Ya played their own music alongside some of their inspirations, other artists who blurred the distinction between the mediums of art and sound.

And then, the piece-de-resistance. On a circular stage, surrounded by chairs, the group loved each other, passionately and disgracefully. They lay bared for the world to see, covering themselves in paint, kissing and spreading their bodies on the canvas. Soon, paint wasn't the only thing smearing across the blank white sheet as nails clawed backs and dripped tiny spots of red, sweat gathered in creases diluting the paint into a strange yellow, and later sheaths of white splattered onto stomachs and backs, and their art was completed. It was filth. It was poetry. What they aimed for wasn't just visual but psychological. *Theatre* as Rev saw it, but no, more than this because despite it being fabricated, it *was* real. They kissed, they touched, they came, eyes closing, moaning, ignoring the need for orchestrated choreography because what is sex if not an act of coarse improvisation? Yes and yes and yes and yes...

Creep took photos of it all. Later, they would be part of a new exhibition. At some point, Joe stormed out. Rev was too engaged with her performance to notice but didn't suppose that it would matter much anyhow. The audience applauded. The curtains fell.

At first, Joe had lied and said that there was no review. Later, he said that he'd written one, but that he didn't think it was any good or worth reading, really, so there was no need to buy the zine. Rev bought it anyway, expecting the worst, and Joe effectively delivered.

Rev sat with him by the kitchen table, hoping that the wait would make him anxious as she read the review in front of him. She hoped that Joe noticed the complete absence of sound, was feeling it under his skin. Rev stared at the page long after she'd finished reading for the sole purpose of elongating this discomfort. The review was, as expected, insulting.

"You imbecile," Rev shouted, perhaps too harshly. She didn't know whether it was best to pretend to lose her temper or maintain an illusion of calm, so decided to embrace the rage, throwing back her chair and pacing as she shouted. "Imbecile, imbecile, imbecile! You didn't think to show me first? The person who allows you to live here, free of board?"

In response, Joe shrugged.

"You're done now." Rev laughed, loudly, insincerely, hoping to emphasise the breadth of her hysteria. "And if you think Tracy will ever forgive you for letting me down…"

"Tracy said it was good. Said I should send it out before I change my mind."

"Oh, did she?" Rev mocked.

"Yeah?"

"HA!" she faltered. "Useless *and* delusional."

Joe kept his eyes down, which bothered her all the more. The truth was, Rev was affronted. Tracy had been drifting for a while now. They were supposed to be the innovators, the pioneers of the group, but seeing her value others over Rev had been painful at first and then devastating when she realised it wasn't going to stop. There was no awe or amazement when Tracy listened to the music now, and sometimes Rev could feel the non-existent eyeroll emitting from her aura.

It was only since Joe arrived that she'd started acting free again.

Tracy knew Rev better than anyone else did. She'd seen her vulnerable and shaken, in every stage of euphoria and distress. They loved each other. Open, untraditional love, but love all the same. Something about Tracy screamed of revolution, which made Rev feel as though she was smitten and giddy for the first time again. It was in the slope of her neck, the way she kicked her legs when she was concentrating, the stubbornness coated in a thick layer of irony... Now, she was slipping away, throwing her approval on gorgeous teenagers. Rev had no chance of competing. Beauty was something she could only access abstractly.

This had been the biggest cause for her regret. It wasn't that Joe was mardy or sullen, nor that he downright refused to do anything remotely creative. It was the fact that he'd stolen Tracy from her, dangled her pathetically as a bargaining chip, silent and unflinching.

"You can leave," Rev told Joe, lighting a cigarette. "It's time for you to go."

Joe shrugged in response. "Nowhere to go."

Rev laughed, exhaling smoke. "I'm afraid that isn't my problem, dear."

"You said everyone was welcome. That they didn't need an invite."

"What you don't realise, Joe, is that we're a community. Frankly, that's something you've never understood."

Prostitution

"Please," Joe scoffed, attempting his usual sulking persona, but Rev could see his eyes were getting wet. He opened his mouth as if he wanted to say something else but closed it again. A second later he muttered another "please," and this time, his voice did crack. Rev was glad to hear it. She tapped her cigarette into the ashtray and let them sit in silence.

When Joe left the squat, the other artists watched through the window. Gypsy sobbed the entire time, black mascara staining her cheeks, but Rev was firm in her conviction. Thankfully, Tracy hadn't argued. She watched Joe leave with arms folded, staring after him with a look in her eyes that Rev knew was dangerous. She snaked her arm over Tracy's shoulders, hoping that them standing together would demonstrate solidarity, a return to tradition.

"It pains me too, but there was simply no other option," Rev said, her eyes on Gypsy but her words intended mostly for Tracy. "Sadly, the only thing that boy could do was be beautiful."

Truism #6:
Labour is a Life-destroying Activity

Judith eventually conceded that there was nothing un-feminist about having a clean kitchen. She snapped on her Marigolds like a surgeon preparing for an operation—a "grunge-ectomy" perhaps—and squatted down in front of the oven. But Christ, the railings were more black than silver. Had they ever been silver? The bowl of soapy water had turned brown in the first few minutes as she kept wringing out the sponge. Judith felt sweat on her forehead and wondered in what way *this* could be considered physical exertion. Why did housework always make her sweat? She had a lot left to do when she threw in the towel, but sod it, she needed a bath herself now. And what did she need an oven for these days? She never bloody cooked anything anyway.

Mann &
Frau & Animal

Susie was enjoying the re-animation of "alone-time." It was something her girlfriends swore by, although she'd laughed it off for months, claiming she simply didn't have time for any of that self-serving nonsense (of course, she phrased it far more tactfully to *them*). Susie was proud of her tiredness. It signalled that she'd spent enough time and energy looking after Alice and Dave, cleaning the house, putting food on the table. Susie was a natural doter. Sometimes she worried that she'd married too young, but it made her feel grown-up when she moaned about Dave's inability to do even the most basic of tasks. Don't get her wrong—she held a lot of respect for him, *really*. Her allowance was generous, and she didn't want for anything, but still, he'd be useless without her. It was a nice trade-off. It was the way things should be.

When Dave injured his foot, Susie was secretly delighted. She loved to make a fuss over him, kissing his cheek and stroking his thinning hair (which she good-naturedly teased him about but didn't really mind in the slightest). She made thousands upon thousands of cups of tea, rubbed his shoulders when he felt tense, and leant over to kiss him on the neck in that way she knew he liked. But the injury had lasted a long time into their marriage. The gratitude that Dave felt slowly shifted into entitlement, and Susie was exhausted.

It was maybe six months ago when she'd snapped. She'd been nearly at her due date, and she wasn't one of those to have a dainty, little bump. She looked huge and bloated despite the fact she was always very careful to watch her figure. Her joints ached constantly, and there seemed to be a permanent drip of sweat behind her knees. Dave asked her to bring him a tinny from the fridge.

"Can't you get it yourself, love? I'm knackered," Susie had responded.

"Sweetheart," he'd counteracted firmly, "my foot."

"Oh for God's sake," she'd muttered, painfully getting up from the chair, both hands clamping down on the armrests. Susie couldn't remember the last time she'd felt comfortable. She ambled over to the fridge and cracked open his beer. It repulsed her. She hadn't been much of a drinker before pregnancy, and now she couldn't even stand the smell without gagging. Suddenly, she was furious beyond all reason. She stormed back to the sofa, as apoplectically as one can storm while forced to waddle, and poured the full beer all over Dave's face.

The worst part was that he barely reacted until the can was empty. He didn't have to say anything. The one and a half minutes of silence during the pouring had said enough. He turned to look up at her. She stared back at him, her mouth open in shock, her hand still tilting as she held the empty can.

"Would you believe that was an accident?" she asked. His expression told her he wouldn't.

"I think you'd best run me a bath."

Later, as she was throwing his clothes in the washer, she felt the tears dripping down her cheeks. What had she been thinking? Why had she been so stupid? She knew she was lucky to have Dave. He was handsome. He earned enough to support them both easily, and yes, Susie was very young, but she'd always been horsey looking. Her teeth stuck out, and her nose beaked. She'd been teased for how she looked at school. Her mother always said it to her, a glass of wine in hand: "*You're going to need to cultivate some charm, kid, because you're not that pretty and you're certainly not that clever.*"

Oh, but she was a good girl! She got respectable O Levels, and she knew how to make a good stew. Now here she was pouring beer over everything. What *had* she been thinking?

She rang Karen, trying to hold back the tears.

"What's the matter, love? Is the baby coming?"

"No, no, it's not that." Breaking into a sob, Susie told Karen the whole story. "I think I'm going mad. I think I'm turning into..." She stopped. Bit back the word although they both knew what she was thinking about—that embarrassing debacle, the random bouts of tears, the near breakdown in the book club. The name "Iris" hovered uncomfortably in the air like the smell of used nappies.

"So, he made you get him a beer and then you ran *him* a bath?" Karen snorted. "Bloody hell, girl, I think you are going mad. I'd have battered him."

Susie laughed a snotty laugh, wiping her hand under her nose. She loved Karen for this sort of thing. She always made her feel more human. Still, she had to remember there was a reason why Karen had two boys, but was alone.

Karen prattled on for a little while about the way she'd belted one of her lads for bringing home some trollop.

"I always say I'm happy with my lads, but honestly Suze, I hope you get a little girl."

When Dave re-emerged from the bathroom with a towel wrapped around his waist, Susie interrupted her.

"Karen, I have to go."

"You'd best tell him off. Don't you dare say you're sorry. I mean it Suze..." Susie hung up the phone.

"Listen," she began. Dave walked to the fridge without looking at her and opened another beer.

"Right then. Take two, is it?" he said, sarcastically.

"Oh Dave, I'm so sorry. I don't know what came over me. I just… I just…" The tears welled-up in her eyes again, and he relented.

"Oh, come here love. Come here." He wrapped his arms round her, standing awkwardly at her side so that their bellies wouldn't meet and squash each other. "There's no need for that, ey?"

"I'm sorry," Susie carried on. "I really am."

"Here, pregnancy makes everyone go a little bit doolally. It's all the hormones and that."

"Yeah," she sniffed. "Yeah, I suppose."

He planted a sloppy kiss on her cheek. "You are silly," he said, laughing as he made his way back to the settee, where thankfully it was only slightly damp now. Susie knew well how to rub, and she was sure she'd gotten the stain up just right.

Such a thing couldn't happen again. Hence, the final begrudging acceptance of "alone-time." They'd all read *Lady Chatterley's Lover* (or at least pretended to), and Judy had got them all worked up about the power of what she called "feminine sexuality." Susie had felt embarrassed by it at the time, but on her own, she liked thinking about it, got hot between her legs as she considered it all. *Wanting someone. Urges.* It all very much appealed. She didn't know how to go about softening this feeling of heat, but she almost didn't want to. It was like how the jittery feeling from a few hours without a fag can be strangely nicer than finally getting one. But eventually, you always have to smoke.

"Alone-time" went like this: Alice was in bed, Dave would be watching the footy or some other such thing, and *Susie* would draw herself a long, hot bath. She'd sit in it while it filled up, and she'd close her eyes and think about all the things that made her feel warm. Then it was lathering time. She always made sure to have a thorough wash anyway, but during "alone-time" it was slightly more private, a little bit more *sensual*. She couldn't exactly describe why it was so different, but she knew she'd be embarrassed if someone walked in and saw her. The avocado walls closed her in safely, and with her eyes up towards the ceiling, Susie would hold her breasts, her nipples poking between the gaps in her fingers as she rubbed them carefully. Her stomach, although not as flat as it used to be, was softer now, and with her eyes closed, it felt nice to touch, to rub with bubbly soap. Then it was her thighs, starting at the knees and going all the way up. She'd spread her legs slightly so she could reach between the creases where her thighs met her shame. Finally, and most indulgently, she shampooed her pubic hair, allowing it to wrap around her fingers, digging deep, massaging it as though she were a hairdresser's assistant, her eyes closed until every piece of her was covered, and she felt perfectly shiny and clean.

The soap at this point would start floating, filmy on top of the water, but she wasn't quite done. The best bit was rinsing off. She attached the rubber shower nozzle to the tap and switched it on. Starting with her face, her shoulders, she allowed the clean water to rinse away the soap, mingling with the creamy bathwater beneath her. Then she moved the nozzle to her stomach, and then her thighs, and then...

She didn't know what to call it, this feeling. She knew that it felt nice, although sometimes too nice, to the point that she flinched away from it, clasping her legs back together. Eventually, it rolled down her body, building up in heat until her toes clenched and occasionally a jet of warm water would escape from her, to which she'd jump out of the bath horrified. She'd switch off the tap and lift out the plug. There was always a guilty thrill when she did this, like she couldn't really believe she'd gotten away with it. Afterward, she'd rinse out the bath and make sure it was all clean, wrap herself up in her dressing gown with a towel on her head and meander out of the bathroom, shouting something like:

"Goodness me. I could've fallen asleep in there!" in a way that she hoped might cover her tracks.

Fluid

For a while after giving birth, being intimate with Dave had been painful, but thankfully that had started to pass. Susie was self-conscious that her body had changed, but he assured her that she was still nice and tight, and she was happy that the doctor had made sure of that. When he pounded her, she closed her eyes and moaned, fantasising about the things that made her warm down there. She didn't mind the act. In fact, she loved feeling closer to Dave and seeing the power she had over him for those few moments. Still, she couldn't help sometimes considering it a shame that a showerhead couldn't support her financially.

Truism #7:
Anger or hate can be a useful motivating force

"I hear you've been taking liberties with my appearance."

Back in her university days when she was eighteen or so, Judith had this habit, likely stolen from Grace Kelly, of tilting her chin and narrowing her eyes whenever she was feeling annoyed. Of course, that was back when everything was still in black and white, and actresses had that little bit of mystery surrounding them.

"Sorry?" he responded, evidently baffled.

"I've been told by reliable sources that you've been taking advantage of how I look for your own sick, personal gain."

"I drew you in the library if that's what you mean?" His voice wasn't what she'd expected. She heard the elongated vowels and harsh consonants which let her know he was from her neck of the woods, although naturally she'd abandoned her accent years ago. There was surprising comfort in finding a Yorkshireman in London. He was

Fluid

almost as alien as his shoulder length hair, his fairy-ish shirt with the frills around the cuffs.

"Well, I'd like to see it," Judith demanded. Simon shrugged. He pulled out his sketchbook from a sharp, leather satchel, and flipped through the pages. He held the book atop his palm, like a record he was scared of scratching.

"I've not had the time to work on the shading."

Judith scoffed, ready to release a stream of abuse before pulling her attention to the drawing. She tried to find the words to frame her anger, but before she had the chance to speak, she couldn't help noticing little details like the pencil drawn behind her ear, or the comfortable, clunky shoes she always wore, seeming to swing under the table even within the stillness of the drawing. In the top right corner, Simon had written the word *Determination*.

"And what does that mean?" She jabbed her finger at it.

"It was the title of the piece," Simon explained, speaking as though he were confused by the question. Judith was equally confused by the use of the word "piece." She was beginning to feel rather stupid, as though she'd started a fight without entirely knowing what it was about.

"Yes, well. Next time you wish to draw somebody, it wouldn't hurt you to ask for permission." She said this deliberately brusquely, but she allowed herself to give him a small smile to indicate that any previous hard feelings had passed.

For some reason, she expected him to smirk. She wanted him to say something like, *"I couldn't help myself, you're just so very beautiful,"* or perhaps to look at least amused by her feisty outburst. Instead, he looked embarrassed.

"Okay," he muttered. Simon walked away first. It was a shame because Judith was usually the one to storm off indignantly, but instead she'd lingered, waiting for more of a reaction until eventually he'd just turned away.

Through the Night Softly

The dole office always told her that she could make something of herself if she ever deigned to set foot in a factory. Well, jokes on them now because that's where she was. Babs had got herself a nice little set-up. She was only short (like five foot nothing), so it didn't take much to make her comfortable. When people threw out their furniture and left them on the side of the road like a whole load of rubbish, Babs always made sure to take advantage. Amazing the things people threw away. Now, a conglomeration of three different settees were spread out on the empty, uncarpeted floor, larger than your standard single bed and a sure sign of luxury in the abandoned industrial complex.

The plastic sheeting kept her warm enough, and it was better for her situation, easier to clean than blankets where everything seemed to soak in and fester. She only had to leave them out in the rain, and they were good as new. She had a

Through the Night Softly

hot plate (battery operated) for all her soup and beans and mugs of tea. She could even heat up water for a bath, although she rarely bothered. It was always too cold taking off her clothes (a duffle coat, two jumpers, a blouse, a vest, a brassier, and that was just on her top half). It was best to carry what she had around with her. Everyone round here was thieving bastards, so she didn't like to get her kit off if she could avoid it. She didn't smell of roses, but then who around these parts did?

It was dark now, rain dripping through the roof. Babs didn't know what time it was, but when it was dark, she liked to try and get some sleep. There wasn't much for her to do if the offy was shut, and when it was cold in the winter, she liked to stay wrapped up as much as possible. Not that she had much hope of sleeping tonight. The lads had turned up again. Bloody idiots, leaving all their rubbish everywhere and smoking their dope. They stupidly thought she couldn't recognise the smell. Didn't they realise the sixties was only twenty bloody minutes ago? And their language was disgraceful.

"Fucking stinks in 'ere," one of them had said.

"Excuse me," Babs replied primly, "this area is occupied."

"Oh shut up, Babs," one of them shouted back.

No respect, these boys. Why didn't they call her Mrs. or Madam? She supposed she hadn't married, but all the same. She was old enough to be their grandmother, for some of them. That

pretty lad who always knocked about couldn't have been more than sixteen.
"See you've brought the eye-candy tonight. Hello, young man!" She still had life in her old bones yet. The boy looked over, scowling. Not a friendly one, but she didn't mind. Her sense of humour made up for the both of them.
"Best to just ignore her," one of them said.
They settled in amongst the rubbish, chattering together, and Babs heard the sound of clicking lighters and clinking bottles.
"And I don't suppose you're sharing then?" she asked. They ignored her as they always did. "I should call the police on you lot. I really should."
"Fuck's sake," one of them muttered. "Here, give this to her."
"Why do I have to go?" the pretty one asked.
"Fine, I'll do it." The leader got up from the middle. He had that stupid haircut they all had these days, spiked up in the middle and stiff with lard, a leather jacket that looked like it'd fallen off a bike once or twice. He sauntered over to Babs looking as though it ached to walk all of a few yards, and handed over the bottle of advocaat, glowing yellow like acid.
"Lovely jubbly," she said, taking it in her gloved hands. "That should keep me nice and warm."
"Yeah, well, just don't bother us."
"You're a good lad, you are," she said. She was fond of them really, felt accustomed to having them around her while she drifted in and out of consciousness on her hazy nights.

Through the Night Softly

Babs stayed drunk most of the time. It wasn't really much of a choice. It was the only way to stave off the agony. She liked the buzz she'd experience before passing out, the kind of wavy feeling where the cushions seemed secure in the whirling room she slept in. It was the only thing that stopped her feeling sick. Hangovers kept her constantly nauseous, her eyes growing heavy, and her throat permanently filled with mucus (and yet somehow still dry). It didn't help that the boys over there kept smoking their rubbish, blowing it all over, even though the windows were smashed, and you'd think it would be easy to avoid gassing the place out. But mostly she could ignore them, her head under the plastic sheeting as they threw their empty bottles against the concrete walls, watching glass shatter and sprinkle the floor like slices of ice on a winter morning.

Sleeping always involved dipping in and out of reality, never understanding whether she was really where she felt she was. She would drink upon awakening and drink in her dreams, and sometimes she would wake up with a thrill on discovering that her last intake of alcohol had all been part of a subconscious fabrication and in fact the bottle of advocaat (or cheap wine or vermouth or whatever it was this medley of misfits had brought for her) was still full. More often it happened the other way around, and occasionally in the thrashing of her nightmares, she would wake to find the bottle smashed next to her and have to lick away the puddles.

As the night went on, Babs was aware of boys leaving, and yet when she woke, she saw a shadow leaning against the opposite corner. Even with her eyesight what it was these days (very poor), she knew that it was her pretty boy since he always stayed the latest, sometimes sleeping in the corners when the other lads would bugger off and leave him without a sofa to relax on. Babs wondered if she should offer to share her pillows, but at her age, she didn't have much fire left. She lifted the advocaat bottle and drank deeply.

"You're still here then, ey?" she asked. She'd thought he was asleep and was surprised to hear him answer.

"Yeah."

"Don't you wanna go home, love?" she asked him.

"It's warm enough in here," he said. But Babs knew it wasn't warm enough for him, not for someone so inexperienced. These young'uns always had their bags on them, but they didn't know the tricks of the trade. Sure, they might have picked up some basic advice about cardboard, but Babs's set-up was basically a home. It'd been so long since her son walked out on her, leaving her with nothing but a black eye, no income, no child benefits, eventually no home to speak of, that she'd gotten used to it all. 'Course, it hadn't been the full twenty years. There'd been boyfriends of sorts, council flats, places she'd had and then lost, but this worked out the best for her. She was never one to care for materialism much anyway. No. It was her son who liked the pretty things. She reckoned he'd like this pretty thing sitting opposite her now.

"It'd get a whole lot warmer if you finish that drink, love," she said. He took a sip from it, but after shuddering, he put it down.

"Nah, fuck this. It's freezing," he said. "You can finish this if you want, Babs." He crawled through the smashed-up window. These boys always liked to pretend there wasn't a perfectly functioning door.

"That I will, love," she said in the dark. But she still had her advocaat.

The thing with drink was that whenever Babs knew there was more, she didn't ration. She didn't stop and think, "Perhaps I'll finish off this, and tomorrow I'll have the vodka." No, she knew that it was there, and therefore she had to drink it.

The lads didn't think that Babs knew they put benzos in the bottles, but she did. She didn't object. They wanted her knocked out so they could chat away the whole night while she slept, and so did she. She knew when necking back the advocaat that it tasted a little strange. It was one of the many reasons she was always so delighted to see them.

But the problem was that the pretty boy hadn't brought the bottle to her. He'd left it where he'd been sitting and yet with the promise of ownership. She tried to stand up, but she felt unsteady on her feet and stumbled onto hands and knees. Well, her bad knee wasn't going to keep her in

Fluid

that position, was it? It had come loose years back, an incident with an ex-boyfriend and a table leg. So, it was on her stomach that she crawled, not quite smoothly but up and down. She winced. The floor was full of their sprinklings of glass. Why did all these boys feel the need to smash things up?

She stopped when she felt the fragments graze her hand. She would have tried to retreat, but there was still the broken bottles underneath her. Like a cat, she circled, trying to find a way around it, but she was scraping her skin on the concrete anyway. Eventually, she decided to just power through. The sooner she got there, the sooner she could drink it and could even douse the cuts with alcohol. They said vodka was one of the best ways to clean out a cut. She'd just have to make sure she saved a little at the bottom. (Yeah, fat chance of that, Babs).

Truism #8:

Romantic love was invented to manipulate women

Judith sat in her regular spot at the library. It was the exact same seat where he had drawn her, but she wasn't thinking about that. She couldn't see him. Perhaps he'd moved places for today. Perhaps he didn't spend that much time in the library in the first place. Judith had indulged this fantasy of their eyes meeting over the top of a book, a pencil in his hand as he stared at her in awe. But he wasn't there. Not that she minded.

Still, it was ludicrous to throw away the afternoon when she should be studying. She'd convinced herself on the short walk to campus that she'd gone with her sole intention being to read and work, and running into Simon would be a mere coincidence, if it were to happen at all.

She settled in her chair, swung her legs in the way that had appeared delightfully childlike in his drawing, but she wasn't thinking about his drawing. She sat still. She read.

She wondered if a coffee might help her concentrate but didn't like the way it always stained her teeth. If she met him here with stale breath and yellow teeth, what would he think of her then? Although, clearly, he already thought she was beautiful. Her head buzzed lightly as she considered herself, scruffy little thing that she was, managing to be the object of desire. He'd admired her from a distance, secretly. That was the kind of thing that only happened in stories.

Judith had read three pages and paid attention to virtually none of it. This was ridiculous.

She stood, planning to storm back to her halls where she could work in peace, with privacy, without worrying about the likes of Simon and his insolent, wandering eyes. Honestly, what must a woman do to be treated seriously in academia?

Reading Position for Second-Degree Burn

Paul can hear the sound of the fairground rides a little way away. There's shouting from the pikeys trying to get the dodgems working so they can spin the pretty girls around. Closer, he can hear his mates kicking the ball, the girls lathering themselves up with oil in the hopes of getting brown. He's aware that there's chatter, but Paul can't hear what they're saying. He could if he wanted to, but he doesn't want to right now. He likes the sound of the waves gushing in and out, the seagulls cawing to each other. It's nice here. He feels safe.

Paul's mouth is dry and his throat is tight as though he's been smoking cigarettes, except he hasn't, and he doesn't understand why this always happens to him. He's hungover. He can feel his brain pulsing behind his eyes, which is part of the reason he wants to keep them closed. His sweat smells vaguely chemically, and he wants to jump in the sea to get clean, but right now he's too comfortable to move. If he'd brought sunglasses, it might be alright, but he didn't. The sun acts as a big warm blanket draping over his body and face. The sand is soft beneath him. He could live here, he thinks, if he needed to. Then he remembers the winter. In the winter, he wouldn't like it very much. And where would he go when the tide came in? Still, it's okay for now. It's definitely okay for now.

"Shove over," says Kelly, plopping down next to him. "What's up with you? Are you dead or summat?"

Paul smiles but keeps his eyes closed. "Who's that?" he says, rubbing his hand up and down her leg, reaching up so he can tap her stomach and breasts with the back of his forearm, pretending to fumble around like a blind man.

"Oi! Ge' off, cheeky." Paul keeps smiling. "Are you coming in the sea with me or what then?" Kelly asks. Paul wouldn't have thought she'd want to go in the sea, what with having all her slap on. He supposes she'd like the opportunity to hide their bottom halves. That should excite him. Paul knows he should go. She probably wants him to splash her with water, to rugby tackle her into the waves so that they can kiss and touch each other. But he doesn't want to move right now.

"I'll recover in a bit," he says. And he will. He knows that. He just wants to lie down for a little while.

"Suit yourself then." He feels her get up.

Reading Position for Second-Degree Burn

Paul's on his own now. He can still taste the bubbles from the can of Coke he just finished. There's salt on his lips from the air, and he licks them, knowing that they'll crack even more. He feels bad, but not quite as rotten as he's pretending to feel. The fact is, he's hungover a lot of the time, and he's usually a bit braver than this. Last night was a big one, though. The girls had been there. He'd snogged Kelly for the first time round the back of the pub. They'd been at each other's faces most of the night.

"You're real good-looking, you know?" she'd said, half-laughing.

"Uh-huh," Paul responded, trying to get her to shut up so that he could keep on kissing her. He liked it though, that she'd said that. When she went home, he thought about that for a lot of the night, that she'd said he was good-looking.

She's a very pretty girl is Kelly, just like the posters on his bedroom wall, hollow features and blonde hair with black eyebrows. She's a skinny malink, but he likes that. She wanted him to go back to hers, but he hadn't. He'd wanted to stay out a bit longer with the lads. She shrugged her shoulders.

"Alright, if you wanna be a gentleman about it."

"We should go to the beach though," he'd said when she was climbing into the taxi. "Tomorrow. We always play footy there on a Sunday, but you can come with, if you want? Bring the girls?"

"I dunno." She'd shrugged. "We'll have to see, won't we?"

Paul liked that too. Lasses were funny. They always pretended you were mad on them, and they weren't all that bothered, but he knew that Kelly was more bothered about him than he was about her. She'd been sidling up to him for weeks. He hadn't even noticed. It weren't until one of his mates asked him: "Are you gonna get in that or what?" that he'd turned around and seen her looking, smouldering over her shoulder as she went to get the drink that he'd failed to buy her. So he started being properly nice to her then, more because it was what was expected than anything else.

But Paul does like girls. He likes snogging them. He just never goes doolally over them, that's all. Ian does. It's well funny. Paul sat on the other side of their bedroom listening to him as he read a girl *poetry* once. Poetry, for fuck's sake. The girl was as nice as she could've been about it, but she kept glancing over at Paul, very embarrassed that he was in the room too. Paul didn't make it any easier for the poor lad. Really though, it was Ian who made it difficult for himself.

"Thanks Ian," she'd said at the end. "That was really, really nice."

Brutal. And he didn't get a snog out of her.

"This is why you're a virgin, mate," Paul said when the girl had left.

Ian scowled. "Not exactly easy when you've got some knobhead lying next to you, is it?"

"Never stopped me before," Paul said. And that was true. It hadn't.

Reading Position for Second-Degree Burn

Thinking about it now makes Paul feel bad. He isn't sure why. It's something to do with Ian being a virgin. He's starting to think that maybe it's not so bad to wait. 'Til marriage, maybe, like his mum says. He doesn't know.

He wants to shag Kelly, but not today. Today, he's quite happy lying on the sand. No one else is bothering him. Someone tried to let him know Craig had turned up with the tinnies. He didn't respond, but they'd sorted it out between themselves.

"Is he fucking deaf?"

"Leave it, mate. He's having one of them days."

Paul's been acting like this more often, sleeping in 'til late, not really wanting to get up. He wouldn't be here today if he could have avoided it, but he'd promised to see Kelly. He isn't really up for it, though. His friends are used to this by now. They know Paul has his moments where he likes to wallow, but then he's usually back on form after a couple of bevs. He doesn't know why things are hard now. Maybe hard isn't the right word but ... *effort*.

Last night, they couldn't get into the club for a dance. The bouncers said they were too pissed. They'd tried to get a taxi, but they were too pissed for that too, apparently. It was lucky because Paul had no idea how much more money he had left in his pay packet. They all went their separate ways and wandered home.

Paul saw a lad he knew. Course you know everyone round here, but this was a kid that he

Fluid

hadn't seen in a long time, not since they was all back in school. He looked *rough*, and not in the way Paul was, but the way that shows someone's been looking rough for a while.

"You alright, mate?" Paul shouted over. He couldn't remember who he was, but he knew he could remember him. He was ignored. For some reason, that really bothered him. "You went to my school, din'tya?" he asked.

The lad looked him over then. *Joseph*. That was it. Little Joey. Half the size of the other kids and hardly ever in class. He gave a smile that was more like a smirk.

"Y'alright?" he said.

"Yeah, not too bad, mate, not too bad."

It was awkward then. They were at an impasse, and Paul didn't know how to proceed. Joey was standing just outside the pub. Paul wished he hadn't stopped to talk.

"Don't suppose I can use the loo in there, can I?" Paul asked.

"They're closing." Joey lit a cigarette.

"Ah, I'll er, I'll just go round the corner then."

Joe shrugged in response, still looking at the ground. Paul didn't actually have to go, but it would seem weird if he didn't after saying all that. He went round the back of the establishment and pissed against one of the bins. As soon as he'd started, he realised he wasn't gonna be able to stop anytime soon, and after he'd managed to wee, he realised he needed to vomit, and by the time he'd finished that, he felt a lot more sober, but tired and empty too. He staggered off, and just as he was turning to wave goodbye to Joey, he saw the lad he was necking off with. No, not lad. *Man*. It was horrible. He was balding. Kind of fat too, that kind of chubby that dads get when they spend too long in the pub. He was kissing Joe's neck, but Joe kept looking forward just smoking his cigarette as though he didn't even notice it was happening.

"Oh right! Puff are you?" Paul shouted. Joe looked at him, indifferently. The old bloke immediately scarpered off, pretending he had nothing to do with it. Paul wanted to go and fight him or something, but he didn't. He'd just been sick. He sauntered off, but he kept turning back to look at Joe who wasn't moving. He just stood there, smoking his cigarette. He didn't even have the balls to look ashamed.

Paul got home and went to sleep, but he woke up after a couple of hours, and he really needed a drink of water. He lay down for a while, but he didn't sleep at all. Eventually he noticed the sun was coming up, making the curtains glow orange. His alarm went off. He just had time to shower and dress before jumping on the train to Bridlington with everyone else. Kelly was there waiting for him. Guess she was keener than she'd let on.

Now, he feels sick again. He doesn't want to think about what he saw last night. He wants to think about Kelly, but he feels sort of rubbish thinking about Kelly because thinking about

Kelly makes him think of Joey and then he thinks of that fat, old man. What was Joey letting him do that for? He can't have liked it.

Paul decides that he's gonna be nice to Ian when he gets home. It's alright if he doesn't wanna get off with girls for a few more years. It's alright if he wants to write poems and that. It's alright that he cries. Really. It's all alright.

His friends are leaving to get fish and chips, but Paul doesn't move.

"You're alright. I'm gonna stay here for a little while."

"You've not moved in *hours*," Kelly complains. She's not joking now. He can tell she's annoyed that he's invited her but isn't talking to her. He reckons Craig probably wants to get off with her. That's alright, Paul thinks. He's not all that bothered, actually.

"I'm knackered," he says, by way of apology. Apparently, that's not really good enough. He hears them walking away, kicking their ball on the sand. Kelly laughs too loudly at something Craig says. It's really high-pitched and annoying. Paul can smell his sweat. He's happy here. He can stay here for a long time. He feels his face and arms getting sore. He might burn. He's probably going to burn. It doesn't matter. He lies still.

Truism #9:

Random mating is good for debunking sex myths

Judith knew what to do to appeal to a young man's sensibilities. She moaned loudly and ground her pelvis with faux enthusiasm, always to encouraging reviews, but for once, she didn't feel like performing. This time it simply wasn't anything special. She was beginning to regret taking him home until he shuddered climatically, and his weight fell on top of her. He lay stiff as a corpse for a few moments, and she considered asking him to move until she felt the wetness on her neck, realised she was hearing shaking breaths and not relieved panting.

"Simon, are you crying?"

He'd wiped his eyes quickly with the back of his hand. Long hair framed his face as he stared down at her. His mouth was still slightly open as though he'd been gasping up until the very last second. He looked beautiful. Not handsome—that wasn't the word. There was something childlike in him, and Judith felt a tug on

Fluid

her heartstrings as she realised how much she wanted to protect this poor boy.

"It's just never felt so right before," he said.

Oxidation Painting

Gary couldn't believe what he'd just gone and done. Even thinking about it tickled him pink. It was childish, sure, but funny too, and none of that mattered because he wouldn't tell a soul. Some things were better left unsaid after all. That was something Gary knew all too well.

Well, he'd probably tell Dave at the pub actually. Dave always got a kick out of stuff like that (sick sense of humour that one, always whapping out the pull-my-finger jokes and such), but honestly, what Gary had done this time really took the biscuit. Even *Dave* might be shocked. Perhaps even a little proud. Gary shook his head when he thought about it. He couldn't wait to watch Jean lose her mind.

She'd always been funny about germs. Gary remembered her moaning at the sight of a crumb, a single crumb, on an empty countertop. And God forbid if he had a few cans and didn't immediately throw them in the rubbish. He couldn't have a single night off in front of the telly without her going mad at him. *Can't you put this in the sink? Can't you turn that down? Can't you pay me any attention?* God, it was like living with a dog. A dog would've been better even. More loyal.

Still, she was only down the road now staying at her mate's house—that mate Iris with all them wavy cardigans and joss sticks. Some hippy divorcee who left her kid with the dad half the week. Gary couldn't stand them types of women. He'd known she was a tosser as soon as she'd moved into the area, said as much to Jean. Jean had probably gone to Iris's just to spite him.

"I'll want my things back at some point," she'd said when she left, dragging that big suitcase behind her. Of course, later he knew he should've told her to fuck off. At the time though, he'd just nodded. He hadn't even thought about her stuff, but it made up most of the flat, despite the fact that *he* was always working and she didn't seem to do a bloody thing. Well, that was absolutely fine by Gary. He'd sort 'em out good and proper, starting with all that cleaning junk.

He'd thrown them all in a bin-bag: the bottles, the cloths, the Brillo pads. Their flat wasn't clean anymore, and Gary liked it like that. Well, he liked some of it. Probably could've done without the pong, but it was a small price to pay for freedom. He'd get it all sorted eventually after he was rid of her shite.

She'd taken all her personal items, the clothes, the make-up (which she never bothered to put on for *him*), but she'd left a lot of junk behind too.

Oxidation Painting

All them books she had knocking about—Jackie Collins, Mills and Boon, all that crap—she was mad for 'em. Gary could hardly get a shag out of her most nights when she had her nose in one of them things, her little bedside lamp turned on, her pissed-off expression whenever he came into the room as though he didn't bloody well live there too... Nah, they were gone. In the bin bag.

Recently, she'd been reading different books. He remembered that one with the tits on the nightstand. *The Female Eunuch*. What was that supposed to mean? Of course, Gary could never have dirty books around the house. He'd be well and truly scuppered if she caught him reading about tits and fannies and all that stuff, but somehow it was alright for *her*. He'd opened it once to see what all the fuss was about and found a scribbled note on the inside cover:

Dear Jean,

I hope this helps you find the answers you've been looking for.

Here for you always,

Iris

Bloody Iris. He should've known she'd had something to do with it. Gary looked all over the place for that book when Jean left, but he didn't find it. Shame, really. He would've loved to dump it in the bin bag. The satisfaction would have been immense. Instead, he threw in the candles from the edge of the bath, the ones she said she needed to "de-stress."

Then it was the flowers. All them sad, plastic flowers she liked. He used to bring her flowers sometimes. Real ones, mind you, none of this fake stuff that she'd started getting. Flowers had always been Gary's saving grace. If he accidently didn't sort out the bills like he'd said he would, or if he sat on the sofa in dirty overalls when he knew it drove her mad, flowers were there. He'd wake her up coming home from a heavy night, and she'd wander around the whole next day slamming cupboards and muttering to herself, but on the way back home from work, he'd quickly grab some flowers from the garage, and lo and behold, that night she'd be right as rain. Sometimes after flowers, he could even get a shag. Made a nice change.

Them days ended when the plastic flowers came in. White, plastic lilies in the bathroom, shiny green leaves with red, berry-looking things next to the telly, pink bubbly shit she called "candytufts" in the bedroom. God, it was a nightmare. He'd bought her back some lovely roses once after a heavy night.

"What do I need them for?" she'd asked, hardly looking up from *The Female* Bloody *Eunuch.*

"Thought it'd be nice," Gary said. "Might go well in the bedroom, if you catch my meaning."

Oxidation Painting

"Why on earth would I want roses in the bedroom?" she said. "They'll clash with the candytufts."

Them fucking candytufts and all the rest of them, straight in the bin bag.

They didn't have many photos together. The ones they did have, he'd already tried to destroy. Him and Dave had set their lighters to them, thrown them in the ashtray while the flames curled round the corners. It was Dave's idea. He said it was the only way Gary could move on, and Gary had to agree because he didn't want to seem any more sentimental than he'd already been all night with his snivelling and wailing. They'd popped upstairs to his flat after the pub shut, and they burned the honeymoon photos. Jean on the donkey by the sea-front, Jean sucking on a stick of rock suggestively, Jean and him with their arms around each other as they grinned at the camera. It had been the best week of Gary's life. He'd hated all the wedding palaver, but the honeymoon, that was great. That had just been for them two, no mothers-in-laws or fat bridesmaids going mad about the colour magenta.

Most of the pictures hadn't been properly destroyed. The fire just left black, bite-like marks around the edges, and Gary managed to salvage them, shove them back in a pile on the kitchen counter. He didn't tell Dave. Embarrassing as it was, he wanted to keep them. It was time though. If he didn't do it then, he wouldn't do it. The honeymoon pictures went in the bin bag too.

Gary looked then, fully took in the assortment of spray bottles, paperback spines, and plastic flowers, unzipped his trousers, pulled himself out, and pissed directly onto everything. He took the bin bag, gave it a shake, and left the house. It had leaked a bit on the kitchen floor, but that was alright. He'd give it a go-over with the mop when he got in.

Gary crawled into his van, carefully placing the bag on the seat next to him, strapping it in like a real passenger. Realistically, he supposed he could've walked, but he wanted to watch her face when she opened it, wanted to hear the hysterical screams of horror as she realised her most sacred things were ruined. The van seemed like a good place to hide.

He parked strategically behind Iris's hedge. He rang the bell, deposited the offending articles on the doorstep and, like a cheeky schoolboy, pegged it back into the van. He'd wound his window down so he could hear, his knuckles between his teeth to make sure he wouldn't laugh. The door opened.

"Jean," he heard Iris call out. "Is this stuff yours?"

"You what?" He heard her voice, was surprised to find it made him feel upset, that kind of squirmy, anxious feeling he got whenever he remembered something awkward like wetting himself in class or crying in front of Dave.

"I think this has been left for you," Iris said.

He heard a bit of rustling.

Oxidation Painting

"Oh for goodness' sake. It's soaking wet!" Gary bit down further on his knuckle. "Christ, it'll be Gare who dropped it off. It's all this junk I don't need anymore."

"We can pop it in the attic if you *want*? I have some of Nick's stuff there…"

"Don't bother," Jean said. "Pongs anyway."

Gary was still biting onto his knuckles, but he wasn't really laughing anymore. Jean wandered round the corner of the hedge to throw the bin bag by the curb for collection, and he panicked, knew that if she just looked to the right, she'd see him parked there, wondered if he should duck down, but he didn't because despite everything, he still wanted to look at her. Did she look fatter now? Her chest seemed bigger in that baggy tie-dye nonsense, a dress-like t-shirt that went well over her leggings. The T-shirt read: *"KUM BY YA! YES! It's art your child could do!"*

She dumped the bin bag by the drain, sniffed her hands, and grimaced. Gary no longer felt amused. He was embarrassed and wished that he hadn't parked up, that he'd just driven home instead.

Jean did look up and notice him. Maybe she didn't know he had the window wound down, but either way, she didn't say anything. She looked embarrassed too as she held up her hand in a wave, a pitying smile on her face. Gary saw she had some glitter on her eyelids, like a little kid. No other make-up at all, just that glitter smeared over her eyes.

He turned on the engine and drove off without waving, reversing off the curb and then heading up the road. He didn't look in the mirror to see if she was still there. A part of him wanted to, but he didn't. Some things, Gary realised, were best left a mystery. Some things were better left unsaid.

Truism #10:
Crimes against property are relatively unimportant

"I think my drawings belong in a gallery. What do you think?"

He couldn't see her face as she was lying on his chest, but Judith hesitated.

"I don't feel entirely comfortable being on display."

"Art belongs on display. When your soul is bared, people can learn who you are without having to ask."

"Images are too ambiguous for me. Words are clearer. More dynamic. People can gain more from them."

Most of Judith and Simon's relationship involved these kinds of masturbatory, speculative conversations.

"You specialise in politics and literature. Who reads the words you write other than fellow academics?" Simon contended.

"I hardly think that's fair!"

"I just mean that pictures are accessible. A child could gain something from a picture. Some of the first things children create are visually artistic."

"Children read stories."

"Well, yes. I suppose."

"So really there's no difference."

"In that case," Simon muttered affectionately, rubbing his nose into her hair, "we should put words on display too."

It was one of many short and pointless conversations, pillow talk for the pretentious as Judith liked to call it. She'd already closed her eyes with every intention of drifting into a pleasant doze when Simon sprang up manically. He swept aside the bedsheets and started ripping out pages from his scrapbook.

"Accessibility," he muttered to himself. "The key is accessibility. Tell me, Judith, what's something you always wanted to say?"

"What do I want to say?" She sat up. "Gosh, I don't know. Something revolutionary. The problem is I don't know what that might be. My ideals have always been Marxist..."

Simon wrote in block letters: **OVERTHROW THE BOURGEOISIE**.

"Great," he said. "Let's start simple. What else?"

"Well, I ought to say something that demonstrates the power of women."

"**DOWN WITH MEN!**" He hurried to write.

"I'm not sure that's exactly what I mean. I don't want men to go *down* as such."

"Well..."

Oxidation Painting

"I mean, in this context. Most of the time as a woman I don't feel empowered, just irritated."

"Irritated how?"

"God, I don't know. Irritated at being spoken down to, angry at people assuming that they must be more intelligent than I am, angry at myself for having to pander to the needs of men. But also…" She paused. She didn't want to admit it, but she supposed that she had to after that little tirade.

"Yes?" Simon prompted her.

"I love men. Fiercely. I want them to love and protect me, but I want to be happy with myself while they do so. I need inner-strength and outward security. I don't know why I'm so bitter that men don't protect women anymore."

Simon ripped out another page from his sketchbook.

MEN DON'T PROTECT YOU ANYMORE.

Soon, they had hundreds of slogans. One liners stretched into political manifestos, and when they ran out of pages, they used Simon's shirts, his cigarette packets, the back of old train tickets.

"I don't agree with this one." Judith held up an undershirt rejoicing the beauty of violence. "It contradicts our messages of hope."

"Things can contradict," Simon said. "We're not trying to make our own philosophy. This is nothing so puritanical as right or wrong. We're just making it accessible, every messy thought, every unjustifiable feeling. It doesn't matter if you don't agree. People have to hear their options."

They'd thrown the pages down from the top of the staircase. They'd stapled the shirts to trees around campus. They'd left the bus tickets in library books. If there was any reaction, Judith wasn't aware of it. It seemed like all of these thoughts were neatly tidied up by the university administration. Judith had wanted to scream with frustration at their wasted time, but Simon swore it wasn't wasted.

"We don't know the impact our work had," he promised, stroking her wrist in the way he knew soothed her.

"Impact? There was no impact! I've heard absolutely nothing."

"And you wouldn't hear if someone on their morning jog felt unsettled when they saw a shirt telling them that weakness is slavery. You don't know if anyone walking through the library saw that abuse of power comes as no surprise and felt empowered to leave an awful partner. We don't know the impact of what we did, and what's more, we shouldn't. All we need to know is that we did it."

Arthur Rimbaud in New York

"Creep, my love, why don't you ever photograph me?"

Creep took a lot of photos. Creep had seen a lot of bodies. They were always scarred and twisted because all bodies, excepting those of newborn babies, are scarred and twisted. His models were dirty. Creep liked bohemian grit, *"the real"* as he called it. He liked the street rats best. He savoured dirt.

Creep saw sweat up close; he smelt it. It was a perfume in its own right. Creep could tell the difference now between the types of sweat. There was the BO someone garnered from staying on the streets too long, washing in public bathrooms without soap; the smell of come-down sweats, chemical and feverish, smells trailing behind sensations which felt like muggy weather and looked like agony immortalised; then there was his favourite sweat, fresh sweat from heat, which lingered on the skin in droplets above lips and eyebrows, the kind of sweat which indicated later more than photographs would develop. Sometimes, Creep felt dispirited. The moments he encapsulated could only be experienced visually. No one could smell the sweat, touch the collarbone, or taste the lips in the same way he had. Creep could only hope his viewers had some imagination.

"You photograph everyone, but you never photograph me."

Creep fingered the Polaroids at the end of the dark room, which was really just a squat with the curtains drawn. Most of the grants Kum By Ya received went towards the chemicals he needed to develop his pictures, which now mostly lay in tubs, soaking. The rest were on lines, pegged up at their corners. They were coming out nicely as far as he could see. This wasn't a proper studio, and Creep almost missed the dark rooms of his old university, but only almost. The privacy and the lack of judgement here meant he could develop what he wanted to, could work in his own way without the sneers from those who feared lewdness—who, in essence, feared truth. In hindsight, Creep realised it was ridiculous to think he would ever have finished art school. It simply wasn't for him. Their room with the curtains drawn? This was for him.

Creep knew who he was even back before they called him "Creep." His father knew too, although that much had remained unsaid. Instead, the beatings were supposedly about "respect" and "discipline" and "refusing to watch his son grow up soft." They hadn't worked, of course. If anything, the trauma made him more sensitive, and now Creep refused to eat meat or wear leather for fear of animals having been beaten into submission too. His college had known, which was the reason for his low grades and even lower attendance. Creep much preferred the non-academic side of university anyway. He was a fan of drinking heavily with hippies and misfits. He very much enjoyed the dramatic societies.

"Creep, I'm starting to get lonely. You're not paying me any attention. Am I going to have to sit here and entertain myself?"

"My darling, I can only apologise."

Creep looked at the photos he'd taken of Joe. That kid was a street rat, alright. He had the dirt, and he smelt like sweat, a mingling of all three kinds. He was scarred and burned and twisted more than most. Somehow, inexplicably, he'd managed to keep his face beautiful. His eyes stood out even in black and white. For many of the photographs, Creep had convinced him to wear a hood over his head, like an execution victim. Those were the pictures Joe liked the most, his bony knees knocked together, his chest leaning forward. A smiling face was drawn over the sack. These were better than the everyday portraits which seemed sad and disingenuous. Joe did everything he was told, stood where he was asked to, posed however was suggested. Creep liked to work with people, not mannequins, but if a mannequin was all he had, he'd do his very best to make it work.

"We have our exhibition coming up, my love. I'm always concerned that things won't develop quite right," Creep explained. He turned around to face his lover, who was lying on the single mattress already in the midst of a sluggish and pathetic masturbation attempt. "But you're right. I'm being neglectful."

Creep's lover was a poet. He wrote words that no one ever read because he explained a kind of love that no one wanted to understand. Creep's lover had spent most of his life being ignored. Really, it was criminal for Creep to ignore him now.

"Come here," Creep's lover said, "and bring your camera."

"I don't want to photograph you."

"Then I must continue to help myself because clearly you don't find me sexually attractive enough for art, and then how can I be sexually attractive enough for anything?"

"Not everyone I photograph is sexually attractive, and I don't photograph everyone I'm sexually attracted to—only those I find aesthetically interesting."

"Even worse! I could live with being unattractive, but uninteresting? That's sinful."

Creep's lover was a poet with a square jaw and a soft stomach and eyes that made it look as though he were in pain. He was constantly watching everything around him, scribbling overheard conversations into notebooks, hoping to deconstruct them and to find some sense of meaning in the nonsense. Creep's lover was interested in humanity, but Creep's eyes were on the bodies. He wanted to see the pain and primitiveness of humanity, the animal needs and wants and desires. His lover's eyes searched for meaning, the whats, the wheres, and whys, the reminders of what separates humans from animals like the way in which people cling onto consciousness, the ridiculousness of being born, and the unrelenting fear of death. The thing, he argued, that made humanity exceptional was this awareness of life and this fear of death. Creep's lover's eyes took in all around him. Right then though, they were watching Creep while he quickened his hand's pace, exhaling slightly through parted lips.

 Creep sat beside him, removed the hand, and took the fingers to his mouth. He kissed them.

 "I think you've made your point."

 "And yet I'm still unsatisfied."

 "Why do you want me to photograph you?"

 "I want you to think that I'm beautiful."

 "I already think that," Creep said truthfully. He stroked the downy hair lining his lover's stomach, lightly kissing his moonlight chest.

 "Am I more beautiful than the boy you're developing?"

 Creep faltered. The answer was no, but it was horrible to say so, and Creep detested lying. He lived this way, on dirty mattresses developing his pictures with the curtains drawn, dropping out of middle class, white, academic existence, all because he abhorred dishonesty. He could have been comfortable, but he would have had to lie. It wasn't worth it.

Most art was dishonest. Painting, drawing, sculpture—these were all forms of lying. Life was not Picasso, not Da Vinci, not Dali, no. Life was a photograph of a boy in a hood with his knees knocked together, developing in the dark room of a dirty flat—a glass crunching underneath feet, smells like sewage kind of flat—with the curtains closed.

"He's practically a child," Creep settled for instead. This was the truth. He was happy with this response.

"You captured him so beautifully."

"He hates the beautiful photos," Creep said, moving on top of his lover, kissing his shoulder, his neck, his chest. "As do I."

Creep saw his lover's crooked body. He smelled the sweat. They always loved so intensely: this photographer, this poet. What they created between them deserved their full physical attention. It was art, so beautiful it could not be real, and Creep only photographed the real. Afterward, they held each other on the single mattress. They had no clothes, and it was getting cold. Their body heat was not enough, but they held each other's shaking bodies because letting go seemed unthinkable. Creep kissed his lover's neck.

Arthur Rimbaud in New York

"You know that we'll die soon," his lover said. Everything that reminded him of life reminded him of death mere moments later.

"What makes you say that, my dear?"

"People like us rarely live long."

"You mean queers?"

"And misfits, and poets, and troublemakers."

"Oh darling, please," Creep scoffed. "I hate it so much when you get philosophical, especially when you're wrong. I know thousands of misfits and poets nearing their senior years, and they're far too busy rolling up fishnets and painting on fruit bowls to die. You've met Revelations."

"We'll die soon." Creep's lover nodded with assuredness. "I feel certain that we'll die soon."

"I'm very sorry to hear that."

"But we're stopping it," Creep's lover said. "We're taking photographs. We're writing. These will last even if few people notice them. The people who search for them will be the right people, those who deserve to know the truth."

"We're making truth."

"But poems are so open to interpretation, and so often misunderstood. I don't think I want to write anymore, my love. I think that it's time I finished with this parody of truth-telling. I want to be immortalised before I die. No one could make a picture of me in the same way you could."

Creep felt the body he held shivering. He stroked the torso side. He thought. He pondered. He abandoned integrity. Creep was an artist with

Fluid

a pathological need to show the real, but more importantly, Creep was deeply, deeply in love.

Over the next few years, he took pictures. Thousands of pictures, his lover sitting, standing, outside, inside, naked, clothed, young and healthy, young and sick, the same sad eyes that wandered and tried to take in all of humanity stared out from a million black and white shots. Film paper curled and crinkled around the edges. This was life. Everything about Creep's lover was life, life cut short, but life lived exceptionally. Creep photographed him in the hospital. He photographed the gravestone. He kept these all together, and he kept them to himself, and then eventually, when he had the guts to share them, people said that they were only portraits. They did not hold the same intensity as his other work. Really, critics argued, Creep's artistic career peaked during his youth in the 70s. Creep's lover's photographs survived in niche art circles among those who found them sentimental yet visceral. Creep loved them because they were real. Creep was not a street rat. Creep was a middle-class, failed academic, and in his lifetime he loved openly and painfully sincerely. This, more than anything else, was his truth.

In a fantastical dark room in a dirty squat, lying naked between crumpled painting sheets and stolen blankets, Creep's lover stared at the camera for the first time.

"Should I smile?" he asked.

"Do whatever you want."

And so, Creep began to make art.

Truism #11:
You can't expect people to be something they're not

It was biting cold. Judith was wrapped in her comfortable coat with thick fur on the inside, and she was still frozen. She could feel the skin between her fingers cracking as she clenched them in her pockets. Her breath was visible in the air like clouds of cigarette smoke, and she was giddy. Soon, she would crawl back into bed with Simon who was currently keeping the sheets warm. She always joked that he was far too lazy, but Judith had grown accustomed to the way she'd return from morning lectures and find him still asleep. She'd crawl next to him, coat and all, until it grew too warm, and the clothes would come off piece by piece, and he would gradually arise too, and soon they would be drowsy, skin to skin with her breath still tasting like her last cup of black coffee and his like sour air, and it wouldn't seem to matter one jot that it was nearly noon, and here they were in bed. It felt like the most natural way to spend their time together.

Fluid

She thumped up the stairs to her dorm room in clunky, black shoes and unlocked the bedroom door. There was Simon. He wasn't in bed. He was looking down at himself in Judith's clothes, trying to cinch his waist thin with his own leather belt, and the worst part was that it was working. With his long hair and thin frame, there was something feminine in him. Perhaps something more feminine than there was in Judith with her shapeless coat, her clunky shoes, her fingernails unpainted and framed with flaking skin. They looked at each other in horror. Simon tried to play it off as a joke.

"Don't you think it becomes me?" he'd said. *Becomes me.* As though he were in some 19th century novel. Judith felt sick. This wasn't something he'd intended to include her in. He'd hidden this, although for how long she couldn't be sure. To laugh now would be a farce.

"Simon, take off my things."

He did. A wise man would have redressed in silence. "It's not what you think anyway. I'm not some kind of fruitcake. Well, anyway, who knows? So many people are these days, I suppose it's tough to say. Isn't everyone a little queer after all? It's not really worth discussing. Everyone has their vices, and it really means nothing to me, nothing at all, and anyway, if you think about those things we said in the truisms…"

"Simon, I'd like you to leave now." He was fully dressed. The only thing left was his coat, hanging on the back of her chair.

"Fine, I suppose you think that's reasonable." He laughed again, a nervous titter which served to emphasise rather than quieten the atmosphere of discomfort. "I think you're making such a mountain out of a molehill but still…"

She stared at him, but she kept her eyes blank and loveless. She didn't want him to think that she felt anything. She didn't want to feel anything.

"Judith, this is who I am."

Simon stood depleted. His eyes were searching hers for something: love, support, affection, something. She longed to hold him. Instinctively, she wanted to lie down with him, let him place his head on her stomach while she stroked his hair. She wanted him to cry so she could tell him it would be okay, wanted him to hurt so she could fix it. Her gut ached to care for this poor child, but humiliation flushed hot within her. She was his lover, not his mother. How had she been so badly mistaken? She thought of her wide hips, her heavy breasts. Had she repulsed him this whole time? She heard her voice more than controlled it.

"You don't have the pride to be a man, nor the means to be a woman. Now leave."

Simon left without his coat. Judith considered chasing him down the stairs to give it back, one final act of kindness. Perhaps she might throw it after him, a final hurrah of hatefulness, but she didn't. She knew how cold it was outside. She knew how he would suffer. She stood by her window. The condensation frosted the corners of the glass, creating a border around her. If Simon looked up, he'd see her framed like a portrait. He didn't. He walked with his head down, his arms wrapped around himself. He never collected his coat. She never ran into him again. A year later, Judith fell into a liaison with one of her lecturers, became pregnant with Tracy, and had to leave. Her parents were hideously angry with her. She wished that she could find Simon who would undoubtedly have been kind to her about the situation, but she simply had no way of knowing where to write. It was too easy for someone like poor Simon to disappear.

Untitled (Self Portrait with Blood)

Apparently it was cold, but Mary couldn't feel it. Perhaps she was warm from all the love and generosity. More likely, it was all the jumpers she'd nicked. The year was creeping into October, and while the sky was bright and the air fresh, biting chills were starting to take effect. According to news reports, this upcoming winter would be a bad one, and Mary and Hannah were contributing to a giveaway outside a multi-faith community centre which the girls had nicknamed "The Church." *The* church because it wasn't *their* church, and this had been cause for concern.

"Why do you need to involve yourself?" their father had asked. "Those people aren't believers."

"It's charity work, Dad," Hannah said. "It's all for a good cause, and Mary will stay with me the whole time."

Mary stood silently, her hands clasped behind her back, hoping she looked sweet or coy, although her father wasn't taking too kindly to sweetness these days. He acted as though it were a sign of insolence whenever Mary behaved exactly in the same way she had since childhood, and now she was unsure whether to stand with good posture or kiss him on the cheek when saying goodbye. It was best to let her sister's blandness speak for the both of them.

He waved his hand to indicate consent, and cautiously, the girls picked up their boxes, both in silence so he wouldn't change his mind.

Outside the church, a sign was jabbed into the grass reading: "Take what you want. Pay what you can." Tables were scattered higgledy-piggledy along the slight incline of the grass, and a variety of sects were attempting to out-do each other's generosity. Mary cartwheeled beside their wobbly table.

"Can you help?" Hannah said, starting to get irritated as she stacked the shawls and jumpers into piles.

"Well, I said we should spread them out so that people could see what they looked like, but you said that was a stupid idea so I'm not helping anymore."

"It doesn't matter what they look like, Mary. This isn't about fashion. It's about *warmth*."

"Well if I'm so thick, you don't need my help then, do you?"

Mary did a handstand and tried to stay upright. Her long skirts floated down from her waist, so Hannah knocked her over, fearing a

Untitled (Self Portrait with Blood)

flash of underwear. Mary screamed insincerely as she fell.

"Goodness sake, you always have to make such a spectacle of yourself," Hannah said. Mary shrugged and started pulling the grass out of the ground. This wasn't as fun as she'd expected. There was no one exciting or interesting here. Some nice, old ladies had made an effort to speak to her.

"You've got lovely, thick curls," they'd said.
"And hasn't she some gams on her?"
"Up to her neck, I'd say!"
"How old are you, love?"
"Fifteen." Mary had been smiling.
"Ooh, and breaking hearts soon enough, I'm sure."

Mary liked the old ladies in their long coats and beanie hats. She liked how they sang in high-pitched voices before calling over to each other in booming Yorkshire accents. Looking over to their cake stall, Mary yearned for their attention. She touched the mad explosion of curls growing sandy and thick out of her head, but it didn't give her the same scalp-tingling sensation as when others touched her. Hannah had long hair too, but hers was flat and fine, sticking to her head like it'd been poured on top. Their father had wanted to cut their hair in order to dissuade vanity, but Hannah begged him not to, and if Hannah got to keep her hair, then so did Mary.

Exhausted mothers dragged around their children, looking for clothes they could get for cheap. They were all embarrassed to be there. Mary could tell. They made excuses, said things like: "Well, I suppose I can chuck you a few bob if it's all for a good cause," while their kids sulked in ugly clothes far too big for them.

Hannah was handing out shawls to the people who came up to their table but refused to engage in conversation. After around half an hour, everyone avoided them. Mary was so used to her regular church members with their disingenuous grins that Hannah's firmness could be refreshing. Right then though, it was dull as sin.

Mary lay on her back, craving sunlight. All the jumpers she'd stolen weren't protecting her from the wind anymore. Some of the sandwich and pie stalls were packing up, and Mary would've wanted to go home too had Hannah not insisted on staying 'til the bitter end. Despite seeming miserable wherever she went, Hannah always insisted on staying 'til the bitter end.

Mary heard their voices before she opened her eyes. They blew in while everyone else was still chatting over Styrofoam coffee cups. She sat up to look at them, but already she could feel Hannah's eyes boring into the back of her head. Mary tried her best to ignore it.

Untitled (Self Portrait with Blood)

The man wasn't tall, but he felt tall. His beard covered half his face, but he was young, no wrinkles round the eyes. The women around him were devastatingly beautiful, dancing in crop tops and baggy trousers despite the freezing cold. They could all sing, which seemed amazing, no bum notes or awkward warbling. And he, surrounded by their beauty, absorbed it, became the sun in their small, little solar system.

He wasn't the only man. There were others, all grinning and still singing as they unloaded the boxes from the van. The group weren't concerned about finding a table. Instead, they dumped the boxes on the floor and continued to sing. When the song ended, they cheered together euphorically, and Mary found herself clapping along too. The man looked at her then, turned his head in her direction. He held her eyes for a few seconds before allowing his mouth to turn upwards. He winked. Mary could feel something beating inside her and fought against every instinct telling her to turn away. Eventually, she hid her face in her jumper to hide the blush. She hoped that he'd find it endearing.

"Good evening, ladies." The man directed this at the old women selling their butterfly buns.

"Now then, young man."

"Would you care for some literature?"

"Depends if it's owt good." They giggled, and Mary recognised it as just that—a giggle. Not a laugh or a guffaw but a girlish flirtation.

"There's nothing quite as good as the word of our Lord, don't you think?" the man replied. The beautiful women handed the leaflets around the tables.

"Our Lord loves you," they said to Hannah, placing their leaflet next to the shawls when she refused to hold out her hand. They walked past Mary without thinking, but she stood to follow.

"Don't," Hannah said. "Just don't."

"They mean Jesus. That's what they mean when they say 'Our Lord.'"

"They mean trouble."

Mary rolled her eyes. She could tell that Hannah was proud of that quip, which bothered her. She turned back to the group.

Even when they weren't singing, they hummed. Even when they weren't dancing, they swayed. This was the way to do it, Mary thought, with music and beauty and laughter. It wasn't long before they began a different song, and Mary joined them, ignoring all of Hannah's muttered "Don't you dares" as she stumbled over. They played. She swayed along awkwardly to the beat, not quite getting the hip swirling movements the other women accomplished. They pulled out tambourines from the back of the van, made a kind of tap, shake, shake rhythm which sounded more rock and roll than righteous, and Mary wished more than anything that she knew the words so she could sing along without mouthing.

He noticed her. He must have seen her in her long skirts, in her many baggy jumpers.

Untitled (Self Portrait with Blood)

"What's your name?" he asked.

"Mary."

"No," he said. "No, you don't seem like a Mary."

"Mary's the mother of God," she defended, hoping that he'd praise her for her knowledge, realising a second later that her knowledge was childish, basic.

"Yes, but you don't seem quite so..." he paused for the right word, "moralistic. You're a free spirit, that's what you are. We need to find you a better name."

Mary felt a grip on her arm. She turned and saw Hannah with a face like thunder, the same severe expression she reserved only for Mary. Hannah was obviously going to tell their dad. She always made sure to grass on Mary, using phrases like "self-respect" and "common decency" while pretending her father's discipline was all a valuable learning curve.

"We're going. Come on. We promised we'd be heading back."

"No, we didn't," Mary said. "We said we'd stay 'til the end or 'til all the shawls were gone."

"Well, it's the end now. We're going."

"Oh no," the bearded man interjected. "This is just the beginning." He held out a hand to Hannah. "I'm David. Pleased to meet you." But Hannah wouldn't touch him. She felt it was dirty. Not dirty as in grime and germs, although frankly it probably was, but dirty like impure. He didn't have a wedding ring, but Hannah noticed how before he'd had his hand on the small of some shirtless woman's back.

"Nice to meet you, but we have to leave."

"I'm not going," Mary said. It amazed her how quickly this resolve appeared, how it could fight away her fundamental survival instinct when it involved a charming man. "I'm staying. We said we weren't home 'til late. 'Til five, that's what we said. I'm staying out 'til five."

Hannah bit a lip. They'd already wasted time here, already been around the wrong people too long. The thought of being caught by her father while standing close to these people drove her near insane.

"We're going," she said again, beginning to walk away. She picked up two heavy boxes, waiting for Mary to gather the rest. She'd done too much looking after Mary for one lifetime, and she was sick of it now. It was always the same. Flirting, running off, and then getting lost, never once considering how Hannah felt when she was shoved to the side. There were no sounds of gathering or footsteps though. Instead, Hannah heard the voice of the man shouting after her, a voice deeper than she felt it had any right to be.

"We'll have her back in one piece!"

Hannah stormed forward stubbornly as her eyes filled with tears.

Untitled (Self Portrait with Blood)

Mary didn't know the songs, but she had an aptitude for the tambourine. It turned out guitar wasn't too hard to pick up either. The girls danced on top of Mary's now-deserted table, swaying their hips while their ab muscles twisted, arms above their heads then trailing down the length of their sides. People stopped and stared. It was effective. They handed out their comics, which they called "letters," with all the details and meeting information, but only after they'd spoken to them about life, and death, and God, and hope, and love, and freedom, and everything else that seemed to come up with these practical strangers. Mary couldn't understand it. It didn't seem as though the girls ever mentioned what the group believed in. Instead, they nodded their heads at everyone else's philosophical arguments pretending, wide-eyed, that every man who spoke with them was telling them brand-new and fascinating information.

"I think it's all bollocks, me," a bald man was saying to two of the girls named "Chaos" and "Freedom." Freedom stood behind Chaos, her arms draped over her shoulders, her hips pressed against her. Mary hadn't seen such closeness between women before. She wanted the girls to grab her from behind too, wanted to feel this sense of affection. Part of her hated it, though. She saw the way David was smiling at them.

"Totally," Chaos was saying, presumably oblivious to the other girl's pubic bone jutting into her back. "That's just what corporate religion wants you to think."

Whoever had a strong opinion one way or the other always left with letters. At the end of the day, Freedom grabbed what was left in the cardboard boxes and threw them in the air, scattering the pavement and the road, allowing them to fall like sycamore seeds onto the bonnets of cars.

"I suppose I'd better go," Mary said. It was a bus by herself now, and even at 4:30, it was already dark.

"Where are you going?" David had asked her.

"Home," she said.

"Pfft, where's home? Surely home is anywhere you want it to be, as long as you're with the people you love."

As he said this, he put his arm around Chaos, pulling her close to his side. Mary tried to swallow her jealousy.

"That's it!" he continued. "You're Gypsy! That's your name. You can be our little Gypsy, and then anywhere is your home."

"Yes!" Chaos reiterated. "Gypsy. It suits you."

And that was enough. She trusted him. For inexplicable reasons, she found that she trusted them all.

"Well, I suppose I can stay for a little while."

That night, Gypsy experienced something new. David showed her power inside herself that she wasn't aware she had. He moved her insides, touched her skin with his, made her feel like she was something magic, something beyond mortal

Untitled (Self Portrait with Blood)

when he gasped in ecstasy. She was told that it would make her feel broken, but it didn't. She wasn't even sure if she felt pain, though there was blood. Chaos kissed away her tears after the event.

"It's okay, my love," she muttered kindly. "It's just to show you that he loves you. To show you that you're free," and Gypsy nodded while she allowed herself to sob, feeling both strong and vulnerable, altered and alive.

At some point, Mary grew bored. She was hungry, and these people didn't seem much interested in dinner. Everyone piled into the van, and David dropped her off at home. He put his hand under her chin and kissed her before she left.

"Remember Gypsy, that you're free. There's always home with us and God," he said, and she nodded, smiling, but somehow, she didn't feel convinced. Her stomach was really hurting her now. She was ready for bed, and she hoped that her father wouldn't still be awake.

Walking up to her house, Mary planned her excuses. She'd make up something, say that the bus broke down, that she'd had to walk, pretend absolutely nothing about her was different. But when she got through the door, Mary's father was up waiting, Hannah by his side. Her face was white and blotchy, her eyes puffed up from crying. She looked at Mary and the grass stains on her outer jumper, knowing that she was too young for what their father planned for her as he took off his belt.

The buckle hit Mary's forehead, and the pain was so sharp she could only gasp. Hannah screamed as well, and from a distance, it was difficult to tell which cries came from the beaten child and which from the guilt-ridden sister. It lasted a few moments, the beating, and then it was done. The silence afterwards was so intense that Mary was scared to moan in pain in case it caused more pain to come. He left the room after, not saying a word. He didn't feel he needed to. This had been cathartic for him. Hannah sobbed on the sofa, her head in her hands, fingers crunching up her thin hair.

"I'm sorry," she said, not breathing so much as gasping in air. "I'm so sorry."

Gypsy looked at her face in the bathroom mirror. She was amazed at how much blood there was, how swollen it had become around the forehead cut. Her nose wasn't straight anymore, and she wondered if it ever would be. She wondered if the kink would be endearing or grotesque. She wondered if she'd still be pretty when it healed.

Untitled (Self Portrait with Blood)

Some of her hair was matted by the blood. She wanted a bath, really. She wanted to wash her face. It was interesting to stare though, and see what had become of her new identity. Mary would have been in floods of tears, but Gypsy wasn't. She wasn't going to be here long; she knew that. Her home was what she made of it, after all.

She turned on the tap, watching as the water went down the plughole, slowly starting to warm up. She tilted her chin and examined her bloody nose again. She smiled. It stung. Slowly, so it wouldn't hurt, Gypsy washed her face.

Truism #12:
Abuse of Power Comes as No Surprise

Judith wasn't one to cope well with being offended. She was, however, prone to moments of inactivity that surprised her. She would have imagined that upon finding the post-it note left on his fridge door that she would've done something drastic, like smash his windows with her fist, or throw a carton of eggs against the wall, or lie in wait for him to return so that she could rip his pecker off, *something*. Really, she could've just waited for his wife to come home. She had the power to destroy his life. Of course, she didn't. It didn't even *occur* to her that that might be the thing to do.

She sat on his kitchen chair, remembering how delighted she was when she first saw that kitchen. It had seemed so grown up and posh, impressing her even more than the shelves of books that had all seemed suspiciously virginal in their un-thumbed, shiny appearance.

Untitled (Self Portrait with Blood)

Judith sobbed, the tears pouring down her cheeks, her stomach convulsing, which immediately meant she had to rush to the toilet to throw up. She'd been throwing up a lot recently. That tiny bean inside of her seemed to twist all her organs like they were playmobiles, perhaps in revenge for having a mother so stupid, stupid, stupid... Judith cried. Her face was soaked with sweat and tears, drool dripping from her lip. Of course he didn't want her. She was a child. A mess.

In hindsight, Judith was very restrained. She followed her usual routine, brushing her teeth, throwing her things in her rucksack, ensuring the bed was properly made. His wife would be back from her conference soon. It wouldn't do to be petty.

It was only on the tube back to her dorm that Judith realised she wasn't sure if she'd remembered to take the post-it note off the fridge. Then, in an epiphany of horror, she remembered. She hadn't even flushed the loo.

I'm too sad to tell you

When Paul is sad, he goes quiet, but Ian cries. He'd been like this since he was a kid, crying on his first day of school, crying when his first day of school ended, crying because he was hungry, crying because he needed help and no one would listen to him… Ian was forever being described as sensitive. Ian knew it was a generous description.

Ian has heard it all already, and he knows. He knows he's soft. He knows he's a wet blanket. He knows he's not tough enough because there's no dad around, even though there's no one on earth tougher than his mum.

Ian stopped crying in public at around ten. He cries less now, but when he does, he really goes for it. He can feel it build up, splashing around inside him, hanging on like a heavy pot that any second now he's sure to drop, his fingers already straining, muscles aching, knowing it'd be too easy to just let go.

I'm too sad to tell you

And he does. As soon as he's alone, it pours out of him, his eyes spilling over until he's gasping in breaths, but they can't quite reach his lungs. He wants to scream, but he can't make a proper sound, so it just becomes a gulp that he'll muffle with his pillow. But even though it feels like it should be so easy, like he's ready to release it all, it isn't.

It starts with a gradual opening of the floodgates, a frustrated build up that won't come even though he knows that he needs to explode, but then finally, he'll feel that trickle of tears start. The hard part's over after that. Ian steps out of himself and thinks about what it is that's making him feel the way he's feeling, and the worst part is it usually doesn't make sense. It could maybe be the sight of something small but tragic, an insignificant comment, a song lyric hitting his brain at just the wrong time, a shattered window pane glittering on the pavement beneath him, and logically, he doesn't know why, but emotionally, he knows that he's weak, that it's happening again, that this is how he feels most of the time, and the only catharsis he's entitled to is when he's alone, head in his pillow, shoulders shaking, chest heaving.

When he's done, he isn't really done. He still feels it. His body is empty. His mind is tired. Ian knows that he can't keep living like this. When he finishes crying, he contemplates what he's going to do. He doesn't want to die. Ian likes the world. He likes crisp mornings and walking to school in his shiny, black shoes. He likes hearing new songs. He likes the taste of cheese and pickle sandwiches and reading his book on a night. He likes it when he's writing poems and the words finally fit together after being tangled up inside his head. He likes the sadness, even. It's real and pure. He doesn't want to stop feeling, and he doesn't want to die. He just doesn't want to be himself. He doesn't want to live as this person in this body any longer.

Before Ian cries, it seems vitally important to hide that he's going to do it, but afterwards, it doesn't matter anymore. He'll lie on his side, his head resting on his pillow, his eyes red and puffy, his cheeks stained with tear tracks that eventually start to sting as they dry out. He'll face away from the wall. His brother Paul will come in from football or his girlfriend's or wherever it happens to be. He'll strip down to his boxers and lie on his back on the bed parallel to him.

"Alright," he'll say. Ian won't reply. They'll lie together in silence, and Ian will think that Paul is so lucky, and he'll wonder if he should say something about the fact that he's been crying, but he reckons that Paul already knows, and he just doesn't care enough to want to speak about it.

Truism #13:
Turn soft and lovely anytime you have a chance

Another bloody romance book. A maid and master. *Forbidden love*. This poor bloody maid fell drastically in love with this gentleman who spends half the novel talking about war with the savages. They'd sneak kisses by the fireside, his hot breath on her ear during intense scoldings, loving (but immoral!) romps—all the things to be expected from any romance novel worth its salt. Judith detested it.

She'd been thinking about her university days recently, thinking about what ol' Karl might have to say about the abuse of power in this romantic dynamic. Judith didn't know why she wasted precious time running this thing.

"Sorry, Judith?" Iris was wrapped up in her usual aura of apprehension. Judith had recently begun to realise wasn't any kind of shyness but simply Iris's neurotic personality permanently presenting itself through her demeanour.

"Yes, Iris, how can I help you?"

Fluid

"I just wanted to apologise on Jean's behalf. She couldn't come today because she's got the baby. Well, it's my baby, but you know how it is. My husband's busy at work, and I would have stayed at home, but Jean kindly offered, and she's so good with him, but still she feels just terrible that she missed it because she really did enjoy the book."

Judith waved her arm dismissively. "It doesn't matter. Go home. Enjoy your evening."

But Iris stayed, looking troubled and confused, or at least more so than usual. Her forehead creased in pain. "Are you sure everything's alright, my love?"

"I just want to say thank you. I've wanted to say it for a while actually, but there was always the other women around, and they already think I'm mad." She laughed, a little awkwardly. "Well, I don't really know if they do... but. Oh, I wanted to thank you all the same. I suppose that's all really." She looked as though she wanted to say more, but the words didn't come. Instead, she shrugged, already looking embarrassed by the outburst. Judith was so overwhelmed by the kindness she wanted to laugh aloud. She managed to restrain herself.

"Well, you're more than welcome, love. I'll see you next week, shall I?"

"Yes, yes. See you next week," Iris said. She rushed off, clipping along in her heels, her handbag the wrong way round, clearly too mortified to notice. It was sweet. Judith hadn't given it much mind before, but Iris did seem happier these days. There was something lighter in her step.

Still, it was all quite tragic. It reminded Judith of too many other times in her life. Times with her daughter, storming off in frustration, times with lovers stomping over icy concrete, times with young boys who'd been turned away from tea. Judith wondered how it would have gone differently if she'd simply asked if they were alright first. She wondered whether it would have made a difference.

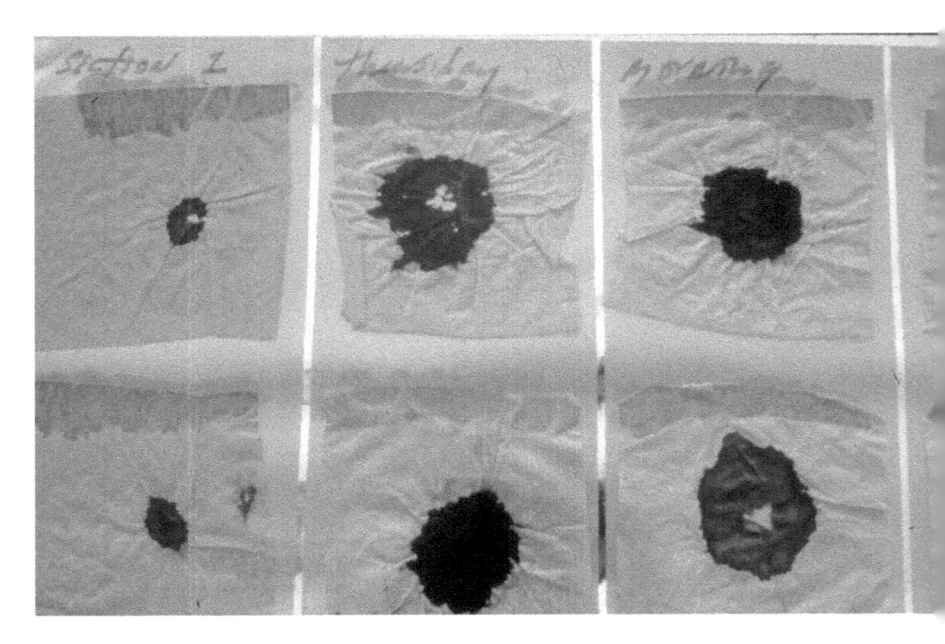

Blood Work Diary, 1972. Menstrual blottings and egg yolk on tissue, 29 x 23 in. each

(c) Carolee Schneemann Foundation / Artists Rights Society, New York

Blood Work Diary

Jean should have guessed it was coming when she'd dropped that spoon and nearly burst into tears. It affected her the same way each month, yet she always forgot about the consistency of her reactions, always just assumed she was losing her mind. The teaspoon clattered. Jean went to pick it up, groaning because now there were brown drips on the tiles which would need wiping up, and she'd have to give it a go over with the cloth first because she didn't want to stain the tea towels, and why would anyone buy white tea towels? And...

"Is everything alright?" Iris had called through from the living room.

"It's fine! You just sit on your arse reading your book, as bloody always," Jean muttered with decreasing volume.

This was unfair, and Jean knew it. Iris had to finish the book for their meeting, and she always let Jean read them first because it took her slightly longer. Besides, they'd only just gotten Nick to bed, and this was the first time Iris had managed to sit down all day. Jean had no right to be irritated, but the burden of her own wrongdoing only served to further enhance her irritation. These kinds of outbursts were exactly the kind of thing Gary used to hate, and Jean hated them too, if she was honest with herself.

"Hey." Iris stood by the kitchen alcove, her eyebrows furrowed in a preternaturally concerned expression. "I'll finish making these. You sit down."

"Alright, then. Fine."

Jean collapsed on the sofa in the next room and switched on the telly. Iris brought the cups through and popped them down on coasters before attaching herself back to the book. There was a nice calm then where neither of them spoke, but both slurped and slumped while the characters on telly chattered away, comforting the mundanity with their melodrama. After the second adverts, Jean took the cups back through to the kitchen and returned with a half-empty packet of biscuits.

"Finish these if you want. I don't like them," she'd said, popping them down on the coffee table. It was her way of an apology. Jean loved Digestives as Iris knew only too well.

"Thank you." Iris smirked, her eyes still on the page as one hand clumsily extracted a biscuit from the packet.

That was how they worked. They understood each other with little gestures and quiet moments.

They watched their Coronation Streets. They read their books. Iris had probably known Jean was PMSing before she did.

Still, spoon dropping incidences aside, it wasn't like Jean to forget. When she'd been married to Gary, there was a little calendar pinned to the fridge where every month she'd draw a little red circle on the right days. She pretended this was for Gary, although he never remembered what it meant and tried it on anyway, despite how many times she'd explained about the staining and the bedsheets. Really, she just didn't want to get pregnant. After their wedding, everyone started to look at her differently. It had taken her long enough to tie the knot, and she wasn't exactly getting any younger, as her mother kept so helpfully reminding her. But Jean saw the kids on a lunchtime scrambling for their dinner, snotty noses and gappy teeth, no manners between the lot of them, and she realised that she was more than happy to wait a few years before bringing another little miracle into the world.

Thankfully, no pregnancies occurred. Jean was careful. More careful than she'd ever been before her marriage, as it happened. When she'd been doing her O Levels, Jean had a bit of a reputation. It was unfairly gained, of course (a cheeky snog after a night out could mutate into an evening of wild passion under the stars when retold through the lens of a young man looking for a little vindication), but as soon as sex became morally accepted within the marriage environment,

Fluid

Jean wanted nothing to do with it. During the honeymoon, Jean realised that the option would always be available to her, and suddenly all the need evaporated. It became a chore almost, a pain. Perhaps it was her mother's fault. As soon as *she'd* started joking about sex, giving conspiratorial winks that Jean could practically hear over the telephone, it was all over.

In book club, the girls were always joking about their husbands and a bit of how's-your-father while nibbling on cream buns and French Fancies. Some of the girls had kids, a lot of them didn't, but they were all married. The books were really just there as an icebreaker. The club was led by Judith, who Iris described as "a handsome woman," all cropped hair and silk shirts. She indulged their sexual jokes with a smile which demonstrated she was both utterly approving and also mature enough to be above it all. They had an absolute riot.

Iris joined soon after Jean did, heavily pregnant with her posh accent and her slow speech, all done up to the nines for no reason whatsoever. Iris couldn't always contribute to the meaningless chatter, often finding herself shoved to the side. But where she failed with the girls, she more than made up for with the books. She said things like:

"I just found the maternal dependency so poignant," and everyone would pull faces like they didn't agree with her, when really they were annoyed because they didn't know what the word "poignant" meant and were resentful to have that brought to their attention. Jean didn't like her at first either. She thought Iris was judgemental and potentially smug. It was only after Nick was born when Jean saw the pregnant belly shrivel into outstretched skin and baggy jumpers, the posh clothes swapped for ill-fitting bras and stained leggings that she realised Iris was as human as the rest of them, even though her husband was minted, and her accent was too posh.

Jean could remember clear as day the conversation that began their shared affection. It was next to the coffee table before the club had started where they all stood with their polystyrene cups, sugar scattered over the sticky surface, and the biscuits tipped onto paper plates.

"'Course, it's only ever when he's bloody pissed that he fancies it, and that's when I want it the least! I can't be doing with a day's worth of work sweat and beer on top of me," Jean was shouting to them all. She was pleased to be at the centre of attention, welcoming any excuse to air her marital grievances. This followed a plethora of confessions from the rest of the group:

"Mind you, I don't really mind mine when he's looking all hot and sweaty…"

"To be honest, I could do with one…"

"Mine's been raring for it ever since the honeymoon…"

And Jean realised that her attempts to bring down her husband had caused a rush of bragging she hadn't anticipated. She was embarrassed and twisted that feeling into annoyance because frankly, the other girls were being unsportsmanlike in their spousal praise.

Iris interrupted: "My husband's not like that. Not often. In fact, it's never really been quite right when we've tried. He comes home late, you see. I hope he'll wake me up, but he doesn't. I suppose we've just never really gotten the gist of it."

The crowd went quiet then as discomfort settled over them. They'd all admitted to not wanting sex themselves, but to have a *husband* who didn't want it was shameful. Posh Iris, all glitz and glamour, and she couldn't lie on her back effectively. It was mortifying.

"It takes a few months to get into the swing of things after you've just had a baby," Jean tentatively offered while knowing that without kids herself, she had no real clue.

"Oh, no!" Iris attempted to recover. "No, it's all completely normal, just a little difficult when he comes home so late."

To avoid further second-hand embarrassment, Susie swerved the conversation around to the benefits of baking soda ("it really does get the stains out, you know"), and Jean watched as Iris's face crumpled, horrified by her own confession.

Thankfully, Judith called the group to order.

"Come on, ladies. It's time to get into our reflection circle." The coffee table was abandoned for the scraping of chairs.

Later, Iris said that if Judith hadn't interrupted, she would have had to leave out of sheer humiliation. But Jean understood. She knew what was meant by "not getting the gist of it."

Iris didn't sleep with her husband, but she clearly indulged her sexuality in other ways:

"There's something so sensuous about the descriptions…"

"I found the ending teasing in its ambiguity…"

"The passion penetrates the pages…"

The other girls would catch Jean's eye, pulling faces that seemed to sarcastically say "I didn't know we were in the midst of a genius," and Jean reciprocated, naturally. The only person encouraging Iris was Judith, who'd nod with her chin in her hands and her lips pressed tightly together. Judith always maintained an intense amount of eye contact, even though Iris often had her own eyes on the book while she expressed these opinions, redness creeping up her neck.

Jean did agree though, despite her eyerolls, that there was something sexy about words which men couldn't understand. Men liked pictures in dirty magazines, all hips and tummies and pouting lips, but nothing wooed a woman more than a well-articulated sentence with just the right amount of filth. After one book club meeting, in her dedicated attempt to keep the flame of her marriage burning, Jean rushed home. She sprinkled herself with perfume, spraying it into the air then walking through so it rested gently on her skin. She didn't have red lipstick, and it would've looked odd on her anyway since she never normally wore it, but she drank red wine for the same effect. She got into her nightgown and pulled it up above her knee, showing off a white expanse of thigh. She picked up the book and pretended to read as she waited for Gary to come home. She even indulged in a cigarette—a privilege she rarely allowed herself because she thought it stained the walls a nasty, yellow colour, which she always nagged Gary about, not that he ever listened. But no, tonight she wouldn't engage with negative thoughts about her husband. Tonight, she was a veritable sex kitten, vapid and breathless, led only by thoughts of desire.

She listened for his steps, for the key in the door, and made sure that she was looking enraptured by her book. She pretended not to notice him until he was in the room, then lifted her eyes from the page.

"Hello," she said in a sultry, old-fashioned voice. She'd copied a lot of it from Iris actually, tried to inject the same level of class into her speech. Jean tried to imagine Gary in his overalls as a saucy vigilante detective on the verge of a breakthrough or else a stable hand, on the poorer side but still feckless in his flirtation with nobility. Jean couldn't remember exactly what he said, but it was something like, "What's wrong with your throat?" or "Pull your gown down. I can see your dinner," and there was simply no point in continuing. She threw the book down, saying, "Forget it" and stormed into the bathroom to get ready for bed. Eventually, he'd cottoned onto what she wanted.

"Well, you only had to say, love. I'm always willing to, um, oblige." He'd winked, and she felt sick and embarrassed at the thought that she'd ever attempted to seduce him. Really, it was a wonder she ever worried about pregnancy. There really was no need.

With Iris, it was different. Jean could have her hands in the mucky dish water, moaning about her wages and the bratty kids at school, and Iris would come up behind her, wrap her arms around her waist, and administer a small kiss to her jawline. She'd mumble something like, "Don't worry about it, darling," and Jean would melt. She'd feel the shivers budding from the kiss and even while wearing unflattering jeans, even with unshaved legs and the extra ten pounds sitting comfortably on her hip bones, she'd feel more erotic than she ever did with Gary and her skinny legs and red wine lips. Perhaps nothing would come of it. It would stay as a hug and a kiss from behind. That feeling would still stay with her all day.

There was no fear of pregnancy with Iris, and yet somehow, inexplicably, Jean had become a mother. Nick was two years old and cherub sweet, built like a Lego block. He was a diamond, but Iris wasn't a natural mum. She spoke to Nick in normal, adult tones. She seemed unable to understand if he started crying out of frustration, sadness, or hunger, and would immediately try to cuddle him while he smacked at her. She couldn't make him laugh. She'd never learned the rules of peekaboo. Iris couldn't shake the horrible guilt she felt about the divorce's effect on her son, although he seemed perfectly fine to Jean. Now, Jean was Nick's favourite. He called her Aunty Jeany, and he clung onto her the second she came home from work. Whenever he'd start scrunching up his eyes as though he were about to cry, Jean would copy him until he laughed. She'd take out a finger in a jokingly firm way: "We'll have none of that here, mister!"

He was sensitive, bless him, cried at the drop of a hat, but he also laughed like a maniac at the slightest provocation. His dad wanted him to be a man's man, but Jean thought there was time enough for that. For now, he could cuddle on her lap after school, he could spoon yogurt into his mouth and laugh hysterically when they clapped. They could make him a man when he was older. Although frankly, Jean was starting to think men were somewhat overrated.

It was late. Jean's stomach was twisted in a familiar gurgle, her back aching in a way she'd recognised since she was twelve. It had been another night of Coronation Street and reading, another night of sweet routine and comfort. Jean was wiping down the kitchen counter. Nick was fast asleep in his bedroom. Iris was in bed too, still awake and reading their book for next week, scribbling little notes in the margin. And here was Jean. Thirty-five. A dinner lady. A size fourteen for the first time in her life. A lover and a mother of sorts. It wasn't how she saw her life heading during her honeymoon in that nasty, Blackpool guesthouse, but she was here. She was doing alright.

She thought about making Iris a cup of tea to show that she appreciated her, but it was far too late, and the caffeine would surely keep her awake. Anyway, this wasn't a night for cups of tea or red wine or half-hearted apologies through biscuits. Instead, Jean went upstairs. She told Iris to put the book down. She kissed her and ran her hand up the back of a cotton nightgown, cupping her neck. Jean pecked her on the cheek, the neck, the jawline. She tangled her fingers in her hair, her mind racing with passion and creativity, and she realised that for the first time in her adult life, the last thing she cared about on God's green earth was the state of the fucking bedsheets.

Truism #14:
The only way to be pure is to stay by yourself

She'd shown him. She couldn't believe it, but she'd shown him.

Judith regarded the circle of chairs, each one the equally perfect distance apart, close enough to add a feeling of companionship while managing to avoid being claustrophobic. On every other chair, she'd left a copy of *The Second Sex*. It seemed like the best place to start.

Judith had embraced the swing of the sixties, feeling like the rest of the world was just catching up on the things she'd known intrinsically for decades. She abandoned her brassiere. She read the literature. She was going to teach this place something beautiful.

For too long, she'd been gutting fishes on the docks. Her new typing job paid well, and her hours were more lenient. Anyway, it would be temporary. Soon, a handful of revolutionary young minds would come through those doors and create a new uprising, Judith was sure of it. This book club would spark a new beginning.

Thirteen years ago, he'd left her a note on the fridge: *I'm sorry, Judith. This can't continue.*

Of course, this was the morning after she'd told him she was pregnant. She thought he'd at least have had the decency to take her to a doctor, to push her towards what he considered to be the *right* decision, but no. He made it patently clear that he didn't care about his offspring enough to even worry it might become a future embarrassment. Judith ran home to her parents in absolute floods of tears, hoping they'd be sympathetic, that they'd understand that she simply couldn't continue with her education, that she needed their support now more than ever, but as soon as she recognised their harsh, lined faces, she suddenly saw herself through their eyes. Judith was unmarried and pregnant. She hadn't even finished her schooling. Of course, she couldn't come home. What'd she been thinking?

She was one of the only women to have studied politics in the institution. Her grades had been brilliant. She'd worked painfully hard. All for nothing.

But no. Finally, she realised it wasn't for nothing. She had Tracy, pain in the arse though she was. Now she had the book club too. Her sign-up sheet had been full for the first week. It was wonderful. She heard a knock on the door.

"Hiya love. This in't the book club, is it?"

"Yes, come in, welcome! What's your name, sorry?"
"Karen."
"Karen Oaks?"
"That's the one."
Judith struck it off the list with her pencil.
"Lovely! It's nice to meet you, Karen. I'm Judith. We'll wait for the others to arrive, but I thought at first we could have a little talk about what we expect from this group and what kind of things we're interested in…"
Karen collapsed on the chair, dropped her handbag down without looking at the floor. For a hefty woman in the early stages of pregnancy, she made no effort to be delicate or quiet in her surroundings. She picked up a copy of the book and skimmed the back.
"And this is the first book, is it?"
"Yes… I wanted to speak first of all about our place in the world."
"Whose place?"
"Um… well, women's."
"Surely that depends, dunnit?"
"What do you mean?"
"Well, I'd say my place in the world is in our local with a white wine shandy, a nice fag, and a bit of decent music, but I guess that's probably not what this Simon bloke meant."
"Well, no, but fair enough."
Little by little, the group dribbled in, some running woefully late, and all of them seeming far more relaxed than urgent. The conversation

was full of laughter and absolutely nothing was taken seriously. Too often they got off topic, and too often Judith tried to guide them back to the point only to find that it was absolutely futile. Still, the girls enjoyed themselves, and Judith imagined that bit by bit she could break them into revolutionaries. Soon they'd be running their own magazines, writing manifestos, taking over the world. Instead, Karen came up to her at the end of the session.

"Listen, this was great and all, but I don't suppose you've got anything a little bit raunchier, have you? When we read 'Book Club for Adult Women,' we all had a bit of a different idea."

Sang/ Lait Chaud

What's good about the telly is that Susie can blather on and on, and it doesn't bother Dave at all. They say it's for women, but he's always been good at multitasking, keeping his mind on two things at once. It was a nice evening. For once, Dave managed to leave work at the door. Susie was doing her knitting, and Tigers were drawing with Stoke City. Dave sipped his beer. It was good to be home.

"I think I'll do a little hat to go with these if I have any wool leftover," Susie said as she held out a little booty on curved needles.

"Oh, aye? Lovely."

"I hope it won't offend your mum, though. I know she got Alice that little white hat at Christmas, but she's nearly grown out of it, and she'll need a new one eventually."

"Hmm."

"You don't think she'll mind?"

"Mind what?"

"If I knit Alice a new hat."

"No, love, no. She won't mind."
"Are they still coming to Alice's birthday tea?"
"Absolutely."
"Both of them?"
"Wild horses couldn't drag them away, love."

Susie smiled, relieved. She always got far too giddy planning parties for the bairn. It was understandable, though. She liked showing off their nice home and her cooking, and Dave had to admit they'd done well in those respects. It were funny because Alice was ten months old and clearly couldn't give a toss about parties, but Susie acted like it was the be-all and end-all to have it go well.

"That's wonderful. She'll be so pleased. Missy was asking me about coming along, but I wondered if it might be too much already. Do you think it'll be too much?" Susie asked.

"You're the one cooking, love. It doesn't bother me."

Dave watched his team lose possession and started to feel slightly bothered by the chatter. Goal to Stoke. Fuck's sake.

"Well, *I* certainly don't mind if she wants to come. I was just wondering if you did," Susie continued.

"Why would I be bothered if your sister comes? She's a right laugh," he said. Suze's lips tightened. *Uh oh. Doghouse.* They had that sisterly competitive thing that Dave didn't really get. Missy was a laugh, though! All the lads down the local loved her. She had a big nose and a big bosom and a larger-than-life personality. Susie had always been a little bit jealous, especially considering that Missy and Dave were both old flirts. But Dave couldn't help it! They were only human. Still, it was best to get on the missus's good side. "Well, I don't mind if she comes if she doesn't get too pissed again," he added, to which Susie gratefully smirked.

"I was thinking maybe we could invite your brother too, if you like." Dave stopped. He made out like he was watching the telly. "Dave?"

"Yeah?"

"I was just saying you can ask your Simon round."

"No, it is getting a bit too many now. He wouldn't like it."

"Are you sure? You've not seen him since the wedding. I hope he doesn't think we're avoiding him."

"Well, he's not really a family man, is he?" Dave snapped. It was quiet then. Dave knew he shouldn't snap at Susie. She barely ever nagged at him in comparison to most wives, but she was doing his head in right then. Not that snapping ever stopped her.

"Well, I think you're being old fashioned, David. I really do." She sniffed.

Where the bloody hell did that come from?

"What's that meant to mean?"

"You know what I mean because you heard what I said."

Sang/Lait Chaud

"No, I don't know what you mean actually because you're chatting a bunch of waffle." It was quiet again. Hull looked like they might score for a hot second, and then they didn't. Dave felt his mood souring. "You can bloody invite him if you want to, but I'll have nowt to do with it." The argument was over, and he'd got the last word, but for some reason, he still felt annoyed.

"Look, if you don't want him round, that's fine. It's just that we all know people who are a bit … funny. My uncle never married."

"Simon's not a puff."

"Well, okay, if you're sure."

Not really, thought Dave. Simon had always been a bit weird, except when they were really little. They used to like kicking the ball about in the ginnel near theirs, and that was nice. They made goalposts with bags and coats and that. Simon nearly always won, but sometimes he let Dave win too, just for a laugh, like. Dave knew it was patronising, but he liked winning so he didn't care. Then Simon held the ball above his head just so Dave wouldn't forget who was boss. *Do you wanna play? Come get it then? Come on! Jump!*

That was right before big school. When Dave moved up to secondary, suddenly everyone was saying stuff like: *In't your brother that fairy in Lower Sixth?* Dave got quite a few scraped knuckles that year. But no one insults your brother, do they? You have to defend them. It's family. His mum was always proud of him for that, but his dad shook his head.

"Why the bloody hell can't Simon defend himself?" he'd ask. And it was true. When people laughed at Simon to his face, he just ignored them. He was always scribbling away in his sketchbooks, his hair over his shoulders. Why did he have to keep his hair that long? No one had long hair in the fifties except for girls. That's just what he'd looked like. A girl. It was alright if he wanted to act like a weirdo, but Dave had to go to that school too. And the most annoying thing about it was he wasn't even gay.

"He's had girlfriends," Dave said to Susie.

"Has he?"

"Yeah."

That drawing Dave'd found, the girl at the desk kicking her shoes, then another one of her lying naked in bed. That was the first time Dave had seen breasts, well before he knew you could get them in magazines. Simon had been home from uni, and Dave was fourteen flipping through his sketchbook. He'd asked Simon about it, but he was frustratingly glib in response. *Oh, well, I suppose that's my girlfriend.* That was around the time he started talking posh too. University did that to people.

"Serious girlfriends?" Susie asked.

"'Course." Dave shrugged. He didn't bloody know.

"Right then." Susie stopped knitting. She stared into space for a while with her eyebrows furrowed, then she shook her head as though she couldn't rightly understand. "Well then, I don't know why you don't want to see him."

"He's not right," Dave said. "In the head I mean."

"Well, what on earth's wrong with him?"

"He does weird stuff, like, he hurts himself. He…" Dave stopped.

"What does that mean?"

Dave didn't know. It was after the wedding he went weird, giving up his job and everything. And the *people* he knocked about with. He'd seen him going about in a long leopard-print coat on a Saturday. Dave had been out with Gary. They'd been heading home from the pub, but it looked like Simon and his group of weirdos were just heading out. What was that about? Lipstick on and all sorts. Dave had wanted to batter him. He thought if he laughed then, that might be enough. He sauntered up to his brother, smirking, and asked him, "Oh aye, stag do, is it?" Dave wanted a proper explanation, a bit of shame maybe, an awkward little shuffle. But Simon had merely kissed him on the cheek and carried on his way. "Whatever helps you sleep at night, darling." That's what he'd said. And he'd seemed so proud of himself, his head held high. He… No. He'd always been a bit wrong. Dave knew that.

"Dave," Susie intervened. "What do you mean he hurts himself?" Dave kept his eyes on the footy. This wasn't a conversation for now. "Darling, what did you mean by that?"

"Look, I'm trying to bloody watch this!" Dave snapped.

Susie knitted quietly for a little while. He couldn't tell her. He wouldn't tell anyone, and he shouldn't have started to. They were silent for ages. This should have made David feel calm, but it didn't. It made him feel even more distressed, and he felt itching on his leg under his trousers that he couldn't scratch, a pain in his temples where he was feeling a headache coming on. He didn't know why Susie always had to ruin things.

It was when Simon's girlfriend had just dumped him. At least, that's what he said to Dave when Dave asked why he hadn't left his bed for ten days, why he didn't want to play footy anymore, why he didn't do anything *normal*. It made sense that it was because of a girl. That's what twenty-year-old lads *should* be getting upset about. Their parents were so relieved it was a girl, they weren't bothered that he was upset. Dave did worry a little bit, though. He knew Simon was dramatic, but he'd never seen him like this.

Dave was fifteen. He had his own friends by then and wasn't all that arsed about knocking around with his brother anymore. Still, he thought he'd try to get him out and about for a bit, get him some fresh air or whatever. Simon was old enough to get the pints in if Dave gave him the money (and during them days Dave always had money because he sold off his cigarettes one by one for five pence in the playground, cheaper than the shops did, but still a profit for him). He'd walked into his brother's room without knocking. Simon was sat on his bed in his pants, not lying down or anything, just sat on the edge staring at the floor, his stupid hair hiding his face.

"Do you wanna come out for a bit?" Dave asked. Simon didn't even respond. "'Ere, are you deaf?"

Simon looked up at him. It was clear he'd been crying.

"Do you like yourself, David? I mean really, genuinely like yourself?" Simon asked him.

Dave shrugged. "Sure, mate. What's not to like?"

Simon laughed, but not in a mocking way, more in disbelief at the simplicity of his response. "That's a good point." Simon laughed again. "What's not to like?" Dave stayed silent for a long time. He wasn't entirely sure what was happening and didn't want to put his foot in it. Simon continued. "The thing is, though, I don't like myself. I don't know why, but there's just nothing. Nothing I do, no way I can be. I can't stand myself. Do you know what that feels like?"

Dave didn't know how to respond. Instead, he gave a nervous titter, trying to match the tone of the conversation to the helpless, disbelieving smile on his brother's face.

"Come on, Si. You don't actually think that."

"Oh, I don't know," Simon said, despondently. "Maybe I do."

He lifted his hand to brush his hair behind his ear. That was when Dave noticed the blood.

"Jesus, what have you done?" he said, rushing forwards and then stopping because he realised

Fluid

he didn't have a clue how to fix it. There was a huge gash across the width of his brother's arm that looked neat and clean, like a deep scratch from barbed wire.

"Oh this? A minor cut. I don't suppose I have the gall to do it properly." Simon laughed slightly. He showed the metal in his other hand, a single blade burnt out of a disposable razor. "See, I did want to die, but I can't stand the thought of being found like this. These arms, these legs..." Simon dragged the razor over his thigh lightly, and the blood spilled out of him like a burst egg yolk. Dave was too shocked to stop him, didn't quite believe what he was looking at. "This face..." He raised his hand to his face.

"No, don't! Please." Dave was angry at how he sounded, desperate and childlike. He was scared for his brother. He was scared for himself. Simon put down the blade.

"You're right," he muttered, rubbing a hand under his nose and smearing a little blood on his lip. "I suppose I'm being maudlin."

Dave couldn't stand it. He left the room and went outside, shouting to his mother that he wouldn't be back for tea. He slammed the door before he heard her response. He wandered on his own to the park and sat on the hill overlooking the playground. It was too late for anyone to be there, and Dave recognised that his skin was full of goosebumps, but his face was hot. He stayed there smoking cigarette after cigarette, waiting for someone to come along and ask him if he was okay, if anything was the matter, so he could talk about what happened, even though the last thing on earth he wanted to do was talk about what happened. No one came. It was too late for all of that. Eventually the streetlamps came on, and he went home. It wasn't really like he had a curfew or anything, but there was something about the streetlamps that said to him "home time," and who was he to deny them? When he got in, Simon's bedroom door was closed. Neither of them mentioned it again. Dave didn't know if his parents knew what Simon did. Dave didn't know if he ever went to do it again. It was better like that, though. Less for him to deal with.

After the game and the news and a couple of nonsense bit shows that Dave didn't find funny, he crawled into bed next to Susie. He was a bit pissed now, and he hadn't really realised it. He knew he smelt bad when he lay next to her. She always smelt like talcum powder and lavender, but she never minded it when he smelt like beer and fags.

Susie woke up to the sound of him crying, but she knew better than to say anything. She'd known something had been the matter. He'd been in a foul mood as soon as she'd mentioned Simon, which was wrong of her. She knew it was a sore topic. Slowly, she moved his head onto her chest and stroked his hair as he let out the sobs until both of them were asleep. They didn't speak of it the next morning, by which point they'd already managed to roll onto opposite sides of the bed.

Simon wasn't mentioned again. Alice's birthday went off without a hitch.

Truism #15:
The most profound things are inexpressible

Judith was happy. She knew she was doing well. She had her little home, her job where she was loved, friends who rang her constantly (some nights she felt she was never off the phone). Tonight it was quiet, and she managed to curl up with a book, wondering if it would be appropriate for the club, jotting little notes onto her pad so she could refer back to them for future reference. She wasn't sure. She'd been told that this book was "gripping," but she wasn't gripped. If anything, she could feel her mind slipping away from the story, not towards anything in particular, just away. She wanted a distraction, for the front door to swing open without her having to get up and let the person in, to be able to hear voices from other rooms without having to engage with them, to live in the buzz of a community, a family, but the house was so silent that she sometimes hummed to herself (out of tune, in no particular melody) just to ensure that she wasn't going mad.

Fluid

She didn't want a lover. Those days were long gone, and she had no particular interest in men (or, depressingly enough, women). But she did want something more, something she felt that she'd already had once. She wasn't sure. Oh well.

Red Flag

The pipes in the squat had been frozen over for the past month and going for a piss was never ideal, but recently, Tracy had been finding it even more vile than usual. Every time she squatted down and glanced at her knickers, she was reminded with increasing, creeping anxiety, that she hadn't gotten her period yet, and it was getting past the point of being "just one of them things."

She wanted to blame the lads, really, but she was angrier with herself. Tracy was usually sensible. She'd mastered the art of tricking Rev, making her think that it was an act of sexual dominance to slam her down and force the latex on, but she'd been less careful with Joe. That wasn't entirely Tracy's fault. During trips, they bled into each other like the contents of smashed glasses, and in those moments, the last thing she wanted to think about was prophylactics. It was all completely mad. Joe still in his teens and her nearing her thirties, and yet somehow, she'd found herself in love. Bit stupid really, when she thought about it.

Then there was Rev of course, getting suspicious.

"Where are those tampons you promised me? We need them for the show." Over the years, Tracy learned that free spirits were always surprisingly keen to stick to a schedule.

"Coming soon, Rev," Tracy would say with her fingers crossed. Then the show came and went, along with Joe, and still nothing. Not even a pinkish tinge. Tracy hoped it was all the stress.

It was supposed to be a joke that Rev wanted blood.

"I'm the commune's vampire," she'd say, baring her teeth and hissing in a way she thought was endearing but that Tracy had begun to find fucking childish to be honest. In the old days when Rev had been Simon, the ease with which Tracy could insert and remove tampons was considered nothing short of a talent. That was back when Tracy still had ownership of her blood. She'd given them to Rev as gifts, who presented them at exhibitions, hoping civilians would see the beauty within them.

"A representation of reality. Authentic sexuality. The truth!" That's what she wrote to the magazines, and Tracy thought she had a point. The critics rarely agreed though, and their "manifestos" were never published. Still, it was a laugh for them to watch as the repressed middle classes recoiled at their antics.

Now, Tracy *had* to hand them over, as evidence or out of some kind of ritualism she didn't know. She couldn't stand it. Even the "sexual liberation" was becoming a chore. Most people she knew were well past that sixties hippy nonsense, but not Rev. Community loyalty was beginning to grate, and after forcing orgasms that would never have come naturally without her exhausted grinding, she couldn't do it anymore. This "liberation" felt less about having the freedom to sleep with who she wanted, but rather a tether Rev had crafted to ensure that no matter who else appeared, they'd always be attached.

Joe understood that kind of love. He'd told her as much when she read his story.

"You called yourself, 'Shithead'?" she asked while reading it. Tracy always felt maternal in her relationships, but it was enhanced tenfold with Joe. She wanted him to be proud of himself because recently all of Gypsy's nagging and faux inspiration was starting to have an impact on his self-esteem. Gypsy had fabricated this idea that she could be Joe's muse, and he would paint beautiful pictures of her and sing her gorgeous songs, which only made him feel bad when he couldn't. All Joe wanted to do was speed or sleep, but there was Gypsy stroking his cheeks trying to rub some poetry out of him. It did Tracy's head in to be honest. But this review proved beyond any shadow of a doubt that he did have some ambition there, and Trace wasn't going to let him lose it.

"Rev won't like it," he'd said.

"Oh, don't worry about Rev." Tracy laughed. "I'll handle Rev. Now send it off before you change your mind."

He did. It was accepted (even though the spelling was atrocious), and Tracy was pleased. But the thing was, she wasn't sure she could handle Rev anymore. She used to have some say, but those days were long gone. Still, she didn't want the other artists to know that yet. For some reason, it seemed important to maintain the illusion of control.

They'd met when Tracy was working at the Red Room as an SS officer. She knew how to put on a routine back then. She couldn't do the accent, but sometimes she liked to pepper a "danke schoen," into conversations, which always went unnoticed and unappreciated. Rev was tagging along to the typical stag-do looking miserable in a suit far too formal for the setting. Back then, 'his' brother was getting married. He'd requested that "Cherry" give him a dance. Cherry was all blonde hair and big busted, so stag-dos gravitated towards her. Afterwards, she stormed back into the girl's toilets (their only changing room) with a face like a slapped arse.

"Watch out for them twats on the front row, Trace. You'll terrify them."

"Will I?" Tracy peeked round the door. She could spot the victims a mile off with their innocent round faces, cheeks turning pink. There were around five lads there with cheap badges advertising "Dave's Stag," and amongst them was Rev, male as anything then in his baggy suit, at least a foot taller than his brother. Tracy noticed him because he wasn't smiling. It was strange for anyone in that setting not to smile.

Her music started: Vera Lynn's "Auf Wiedersehen." She sauntered onstage slowly, seductively removing her trench coat to reveal a pair of leather shorts and braces. She dipped and bent her knees, gliding her hands down her thighs, mouthing along to the words. Then the music changed again, this time to something fast and loud. She stalked across the platform in her thigh-high boots, the heel sharp as a knife, tough enough to walk in, let alone dance. Normally, it was protocol to go for the groom, but the shy ones were always the most fun, so she began straddling Rev, her naked breasts nearly brushing against the cheek he'd awkwardly turned away. She proceeded to grind until satisfied that he was at least verging on aroused, then moved on. The customers were easy to manipulate, and her performance went well as she traced her fingertips over the men's cheeks and almost, but not quite, sat in their laps. She even let someone try on her hat (with genuine skull, no less!)

Fluid

When Rev's brother reached over to grab her breast, she screamed "nein" and shoved her stiletto into his foot. This behaviour nearly always got her into trouble, but she maintained it was essential for the role and usually got away with it.

Not this time, though. Poor Dave bled everywhere. The heel had gone right through his loafers. Tracy maintained it was a total accident, but her obvious lack of concern indisputably proved her guilt, and she got the sack. To be honest, it had been a long time coming. Ah well. It was fun while it lasted.

Somehow though, in all of this calamity, Rev had fallen madly and irrevocably in love with her.

She found him by her car smoking a cigarette. *Uh oh,* she'd thought, *here's trouble.* But he hadn't wanted her body. He wasn't even that bothered about her personality.

"I like your boots," he'd said. "I've never seen boots like that before."

"Yeah?" Tracy had replied. "I'd let you borrow them, but they might not fit you, love." She laughed, and when he looked absolutely terrified, she realised that may have been the wrong thing to say.

"I didn't mean that! I'm not..." he attempted.

But Tracy knew. She didn't mind either. She invited him back for a coffee, which turned to brandy, and they had a good laugh about the night and the ambulance and even the sacking in the end. She even let him try on her boots, although he couldn't get his foot in properly. He started borrowing her clothes a lot. Then he was drawing on his eyebrows. Soon they were sharing a bed, which seemed pretty much inevitable, and before they knew it, he was she, and she was Revelations, Rev the six foot tall Amazonian Goddess in fishnet tights and (fitting!) knee-high boots. And it wasn't just Tracy who helped Rev. There was a mutual love and respect there. She admired her since she had an actual degree in the Contemporary Arts, from what she knew was a good university because her mother never stopped banging on about the time she'd dropped out of it to have her. Rev had even developed a southern accent during her time in academia.

"You're faaahr more than just a stripper, Trace," Rev told her, red nails tapping on a cigarette. "You're an artiste."

So, they started doing shows. Actual shows with a message and meaning, where blood wasn't just allowed but actively encouraged. They began busking in parks until the police would move them on. Their reputation grew enough that they began receiving grants.

In institutes, they would stand, fully dressed, Rev in her manly, uptight suit, Tracy in her glad rags. They'd strip each other down in front of the audience, make passionate, beautiful love, before separating and redressing in each other's clothes.

Walking off stage, looking fairly ridiculous, they'd be laughing.

"You know," Rev would say, "I'm not entirely sure they understood the point of that."

Fluid

Conservatives protested, naturally. The placards read that they were public menaces. It urged viewers to turn to the Bible, particularly to Revelations. It was never really decided whether Rev got her name before or after the shows (Tracy swore after; Rev swore before), but she still found it hilarious to stand in front of them in full regalia shouting, "Yes, children! Turn to me!"

Tracy was so unbelievably grateful that often she wanted to cry. Every time she remembered that she didn't have to deal with beer breath or idiots who thought she was stupid, she felt a love so pure and genuine that she thought it might kill her if she lost it. Kum By Ya was their sexy, sweaty, bloody, soaking brainchild. It wasn't perfect, but here they were.

"This isn't going to end, is it?" Tracy asked Rev one night as they shared a cigarette on the pile of cushions they called a "bed."

"Goodness, I hope not," she replied. "Not if I have anything to do with it."

Then Joe came. Young Joe, brooding and mysterious, and Tracy fell in love. It seemed fair. Rev had fallen in love with a number of women over the years, and it never enraged Tracy, but Rev was livid. The review was apparently the "final straw." It "reflected badly on the commune." It "didn't represent the true feelings of the group." Tracy thought it represented her feelings just fine. That didn't matter. He had to go.

Now Joe was gone, and Tracy's stomach was killing her. She'd hoped that female intuition could help her distinguish between the types of cramp. Was this one sharp pain because she hadn't pissed all day? Maybe a period cramp, finally? Or was it something worse, something terrible, the first kicks of a new life? The thought made her feel even sicker as she slumped father down on the sofa.

Rev came in, in a dress far too young and tight for her and perched herself on the armrest next to Tracy's feet. This was the kind of thing Tracy found herself thinking these days. Mean, judgemental things. Everything Rev did repulsed her now, which was odd because it never used to.

"Hey Trace, can I have a word?"

"If you want. I'm not exactly going anywhere."

Rev smiled tightly, ran a finger through her hair as she inhaled. "I know what you told Joe to do."

"Yeah? What was that, then?" Tracy said.

"You encouraged him to send off that review. I'm sure you thought it was a nice idea at the time. I'm sure you had good intentions and hadn't read it in a thorough manner." Tracy stayed quiet. Rev stared at her for an uncomfortable amount of time, the same fixed smile on her face. "I would have asked you to leave in different circumstances."

"You what?" Tracy sat up, ignoring the pressure in her stomach.

"Don't worry." Rev laughed. "I'm not stupid, you know? I'm aware of your situation."

"What situation?"

"Oh darling." Rev laughed. "Well, I've not had a tampon for a while."

Tracy felt vomit rise in her throat, swallowed it. It seemed more concrete if other people had begun to notice too. She wasn't insane or paranoid. This wasn't just her mad imagination. Her period was very late and she was nauseous. This was happening. Rev laughed loudly and rubbed Tracy's shin.

"Don't look so scared! Sweetheart, I'm delighted."

"Are you?"

"Of course! Who else but us could make good parents?"

Tracy said nothing. She couldn't be certain, but it made sense that this wouldn't be Rev's baby. Rev knew that too. In fact, she looked threatening as she spoke, her hand now resting on Tracy's stomach.

"I really would have made you leave, you know?" she said. "I'm finding myself trusting you less each day, and believe me, darling, that's not what I want."

Rev leaned forward to kiss Tracy on the forehead. Her lips lingered for too long, and Tracy felt uncomfortably hot. She imagined the yellow, stained teeth, the wrinkles round her puckered lips. She'd never thought Rev was unattractive before. Her appearance hadn't drastically changed since the last time they'd slept together, but now she felt sick at the thought of her. Maybe she just felt sick in general. Rev leaned backwards again, looked at Tracy with a faux, warm smile, the kind of smile that seemed as though it'd been practised for this moment.

"I'm not going to ask you to leave," Rev said. "Our little family can be the fresh start we need. Look! Our little miracle has already saved you."

Tracy didn't respond.

The next few days passed, and Tracy kept quiet. She didn't say anything about her plans to leave or dramatically pack up any of her things like she wanted to. She didn't refuse to join trust circles or turn down kisses. At night, she rested heavy books on her stomach, sometimes thumped herself, and hard too, but only when no one was watching. Otherwise, things continued as normal. She pissed regularly and avoided Rev's questions until eventually, with a feeling of relief so intense she could have fainted, she saw it.

There was blood in her underwear.

She found it first on the toilet paper, the slight tainting of brown, then grappled for the pants round her ankles and confirmed it when she saw the jagged, oval smudge. Before she realised exactly how she felt, she was sobbing, her chest heaving with relief, snot and tears dripping down her face. She smeared them onto her cheeks with the back of her hand but kept crying. *Thank*

Fluid

God, she thought, *oh Christ, thank god.* Tracy Lamb was free.

She decided to leave the used tampon on Rev's pillow. With all the "gifts" that Rev received, it was important Tracy left a note so that she'd know it was from her. She could've written "fuck off," or perhaps "take your miracle and shove it up your arse," but she settled for something mildly classier, then left the house with her rucksack all packed and walked away. She breathed in deeply as she left the house. The icy air was refreshing.

Tracy never wanted to see Rev again in her life, but she knew that she would. They had connections, after all. It wouldn't take long for them to be thrust back together because that's what happens with people. They interacted so incidentally, so fluidly that Tracy felt that to swear off seeing anyone again was an impossibility. But this was not an upsetting thought. If anything, it helped her feel more connected to the world around her. It all threaded together, and here she was, running through it insignificantly but impacting on everyone she touched. She realised she was walking and breathing more consciously than she ever had in her life. Not knowing where she was going, she focused on the actions of her body, the breath, the steps, the swallows, and could almost feel the blood as it left her.

She would meet new people. She would run into old flames. She would almost definitely see Rev, but she also might find Joe and that seemed to Tracy like a fair compromise.

Red Flag

It was goodbye, but this felt like a beginning.

Truism #16:

All things are delicately interconnected

"Hello?"

"Hey Mum, it's me."

"Oh my God, Tracy!"

"What?"

"Nothing, I just didn't expect to hear from you after so long."

"Christ, don't start."

"I'm not starting. I… Forget it. How are you?"

"I'm fine, yeah. You?"

"Yes, well."

"Good. Right… Well… Look, I can't talk for long. I'll run out of change. Can I come back for a bit? Home, I mean. It's just, I've met this lad, and he's only nineteen, and he doesn't have anywhere to go. Neither do I really, but…"

"Yes."

"What?"

"Yes, fine he can stay for a little while. You too if you like. There's still your old bedroom. And the sofa."

Red Flag

"Really?"
"Aye, plenty of space."
"Are you sure? I wouldn't ask, but it's sort of an emergency, like."
"How cold is it out, love?"
"Ha! It's fucking freezing."
"Right. Well, it won't do to have you and whoever this boy is sleeping rough. I doubt either of you have a proper jacket."
"Alright. Cheers, Mum. We'll be there soon. We just need change for the bus."
"Get a taxi, love. I'll pay when you get here."
"Are you joking?"
"Are you going to risk asking twice?"
"Alright."
"You're welcome."
"Mum, why are you being like this?"
"Like what?"
"I dunno. Nice."
"Charming! I suppose it's out of character for me."
"No, no I didn't mean that. Christ…"
"It's fine, love. I don't know why. I've gone stupidly reflective in my old age. Have you had your tea?"
"No. We've not thought, really…"
"Wonderful. I'll get some chops out the freezer."

"Execution Victim #8" Photograph by Kum By Ya Collective.
"Art Your Child Could Do" Exhibit 1977.

Frankie Teardrop

(A review)

All this **"ART"** was piss, shit, blood, that kind of stuff. Loads of **SEX** too the audiense looked turned on the **HOLE** time (haha! Get it?) There were music. That were the best bit. Good songs too like **FRANKIE TEARDROP,** songs that tell a story like. (The REV says **stories and art are the SAME THING** but I think s/hes not right in the head.)

Shithead knew frankie Teardrop well. Frankie told shithead about his wife. She knew what frankie was (**A FAG!!**) She loved him and there son but it was time for her to leave. She ecspected frankie to be more of a "hands-on" father. frankie told Shithead this real pissed off like. He sed that the baby were alone right then. Hed just left him in his cot asleep while he went for a drive because every time he saw his face Frankie were reminded about who he was and what hed done and how his wife knew everything. frankie wunt a real man. His marridge was a sham. frankie dint know if the baby was still sleeping or if someone had nicked him. It would be better if someone gave him a home but there were a part of frankie hoping his baby would be delivered on the doorstep, **CUT UP** into bits in a cardboard box cus even though frankie loved his son he knew he were never gonna be a proper dad. Frankie told shithead hed never had a dad himself. His experienses of parenting were flawed AT BEST.

Frankie had no idea what the **FUCK** he were meant to be doing. It would be easier if they was all dead he sed. Sometimes he wondered if he shud **DO IT HIMSELF** and hed do it tomorro if it wunt for shithead. Shithead understood him. Shithead kept him **SANE**.

But the problem were that shithead fucked off because he were sick of the way frankie took up all his time. Shithead hated seeing frankie wating outside clubs in that stupid fucking FORD so shithead left. He found a

Red Flag

squat on Prince Street and stoped goin to all them other places hoping that frankie wunt find him. Cus shithead left he knew frankie might kill the baby. He might have already done it and be rotting in Her Majestys pleasure **RIGHT NOW.**

Shithead worked on **ART YOUR CHILD COULD DO.** They performed that show with **piss and shit and that** and meanwile frankies family and frankie are all dead and no one knows a thing about it cus no one gives a shit. Leest of all shithead.

Is this story fucking art ey, rev? I guess **its all just piss and shit and that really.**

Photograph of original: "Auf Wiedersehen, You Bastard." Kum By Ya Collective. "Art Only a Mother Could Love" exhibit. 1978. Fabric, paper, and menstrual blood. 100 x 144 cm.

Works Cited

Abramovic, Marina. "Rhythm 0". 1974. Tate. London.

Burden, Chris. "Through the Night Softly". 1973. Electronic Arts Intermix (EAI). New York.

Chicago, Judy. "Menstruation Bathroom". Sourced from: Broude, Norma; Garrard, Mary D.; Brodsky, Judith K. *The power of feminist art: the American movement of the 1970s, history and impact.* Abrams, 1994. Lloyd Hamrol as photographer.

Chicago, Judy. "Red Flag". 1971. Turner Carroll Gallery. Sante Fe.

COUM Transmissions. "Prostitution". 1976. Institute of Contemporary Arts. London.

Export, Valie. "Mann & Frau & Animal". 1970-1973. Light Cone Distribution, Exhibition, and Conservation of Experimental Film. Paris.

Holzer, Jenny. "Truisms". 1978-87. Museum of Modern Art. New York.

Jan Ader, Bas. "I'm Too Sad to Tell You". 1971. Simon Lee Gallery. London.

Kelly, Mary. "Post-Partum Document: Documentation I, Analysed Faecal Stains and Feeding Charts". 1974. Perspex unit, white card, diaper linings, plastic, sheeting, paper, ink. Detail, 1 of 31 units, 28 x 35.5 cm. Art Gallery of Ontario. Ontario.

Mendieta, Ana. "Untitled: (Self-Portrait with Blood". 1973. Tate. London.

Oppenheim, Dennis. "Reading Position for Second-Degree Burn". 1970. IMMA Collection: Donated by the artist, 2001. Dublin.

Pane, Gina. "Action Le Lait Chaud". 1972. Centre Pompidou. Paris.

Schneemann, Carolee. "Blood Work Diary". 1972. PPOW Gallery. New York. Image: *Blood Work Diary*, 1972. Menstrual blottings and egg yolk on tissue, 29 x 23 in. each

(c) Carolee Schneemann Foundation / Artists Rights Society, New York

Works Cited

Warhol, Andy. "Oxidation Paintings". 1978. Collection Norman and Norah Stone, San Francisco. The Andy Warhol Foundation for the Visual Arts, Inc., NY.

Westwood, Vivienne. "Two Cowboys Handkerchief". 1974-75. The Metropolitan Museum of Art. New York.

Wojnarowicz, David. "Arthur Rimbaud in New York". 1978-79. Courtesy of PPOW Gallery, NY and the Estate of David Wojnarowicz.

Book Club Questions

Hey-oh! If you're in a book club, you've come to the right place. What a book to choose! Why not have a book club where we can talk about a book about a book club? Surely, this is meta-genius! And if not and you're sitting in your bedroom on your own looking at the back tat then, ah well. Let's just embrace your inner Judith and get thoughtful for a moment:

1) What connections lie between artistic mediums? Do you agree with Revelation and Judith's idea that words should be on display? How about Creep and his lover's idea that pictures are more honest than words?

2) Why do you think there was so much use of body fluids within artwork in this particular historical period? What were so many

artists attempting to say with abjection and disgust?

3) How does gender work within these stories? Is this book feminist? Trans-inclusive? As the writer I would like to hope so, but where do the problematic elements lie? How might this change if it were set in present times?

4) Why do you think the characters felt drawn to *Kum By Ya*? What was so special about that community?

5) What role does maternity play within this novel? Paternity?

6) Why was the Freudian significance so poignant? (This is a joke).

Author Bio

Cathleen Davies is a writer from East Yorkshire. Their work has appeared in various magazines and anthologies. Their debut collection of short-stories *Cheeky, Bloody Articles* was published by 4Horsemen in 2022. This is their second solo publication.

More Books from 4 Horsemen Publications

Literary & Short Story Collections

Cathleen Davies
Cheeky, Bloody Articles

Anthologies & Collections

4HP Anthologies
Teen Angst: Mix Vol. 1
Teen Angst: Mix Vol. 2
My Wedding Date
The Offices of Supernatural Being
The Sentient Space

Demonic Anthologies
Demonic Wildlife
Demonic Household
Demonic Carnival
Demonic Classics
Demonic Vacations
Demonic Medicine
Demonic Workplace
& more to follow!

XXX- Holiday Collection
Unwrap Me
Stuffing My Stocking

Coloring Books

Jenn Kotick
Mermaids

Discover more at
4HorsemenPublications.com

Milton Keynes UK
Ingram Content Group UK Ltd.
UKHW011543010224
436956UK00004B/15